SALLY

PEGGY FIELDING

*Dear Mary ~ tender
thanks for the
moments
love
Peggy Fielding*

Hard Shell Word Factory

For Miss Hazel, who was shocked by the whole thing.

© 2001, Peggy Fielding
ISBN: 0-7599-0330-1
Trade Paperback
Published August 2001
Ebook ISBN: 0-7599-0329-8
Published July 2001

Hard Shell Word Factory
PO Box 161
Amherst Jct. WI 54407
Cover art © 2001

AUTHOR'S NOTE

SALLY is a novel, so it is therefore fiction.

I have tried to tell Sally Hemings' story as honestly as I could, considering the scanty information available. I've tried to use accurate dates to head the chapters. In every case where there is historical proof of a happening in Sally's life during the years that this book covers, youth to her first baby, that material has been included in the story. The rest is what I imagined happened. Since her grandmother was brought from Africa, I also incorporated the occult overtones and the special African learnings that Sally might have received from that grandmother via her mother, Betsy Hemings.

I studied several historical accounts of the Jefferson years but finally settled upon Fawn M. Brodie's book, THOMAS JEFFERSON; AN INTIMATE BIOGRAPHY as my main research tool.

I only hope readers will learn to know and love Sally as I learned to know and love her in the writing.

Peggy Fielding

Chapter One

July 1833

AT THE WINDOW of the small rented house, Sally Hemings stood transfixed, staring out across the field as if watching a scene being played out for her and for her alone.

Madison Hemings looked intently at his mother's preoccupied stance. When it became clear that she wasn't going to notice that he was in the room he moved to stand behind her. He put his hand on her shoulder and felt her start of surprise. Through one of the squares of glass above her head he could see a slightly distorted vista of the green rolling hills of Albemarle County, Virginia. Beautiful, of course, but certainly nothing new to a woman who had lived in the area almost all her life.

"What are you looking for, Mother?"

His mother continued to stare out but she murmured a few words toward the glass.

"He died eight years ago today."

He! Madison didn't have to ask who she was speaking of. He! Ready to shout with anger, he reminded himself of his own ambivalence toward the man who had been his father, the man who had kept him listed on the plantation roles as a slave until he was 21. He made an effort to keep his voice from betraying his rage.

"Mother, that was a long time ago. You're not still mourning the old man, are you?" He looked down into his mother's face.

She put up her hand and smiled up at his freckled visage as if by smiling she could cut off any further examination. He returned her protective ploy with a smile of his own and a probing question.

"Tell me, Mistress Sally, would you really rather be a slave again?"

The sadness he read in Sally Heming's brown eyes and even more in her smile caused Madison to take pity. He let his voice soften in sympathy.

"Oh, I know. Sometimes I get hungry to see home again, too. But

Mother, nothing is the same. It's been three years since they sold the place."

"I know you don't understand this, Madison, but I want to see our old home once more before I die. It's the place where you were born. I should think you and your brother would wish to see it also."

Madison Hemings glanced again at the green Virginia countryside.

"Some tell me that all is dilapidation and ruin on the little mountain, Mother." He placed his arm about her shoulders and turned her away from the window.

"Perhaps so. I suppose I've heard the same stories you've heard. That's one of the reasons I will visit Monticello once more. Can we not go there together, son?"

The tall young man sighed and bent to touch his lips to the still smooth cheek of his sixty-two-year-old mother.

"You're a woman who cannot be denied. We will go together, madam. When did you wish to set out upon this long tour?"

"Is the trip to Monticello such a chore for you, my son?"

"My life at Monticello was not all sunshine and happiness, Mother. As you know well. A slave is a slave, no matter how light his duties." Madison again felt the old bleakness, the old longing to be "accepted" again invade his soul. "None of us ever really knew our father, you know. Not really." He shook her calico-clad shoulder lightly, "Maybe not even you. I'm willing to wager that not even his white family really knew that old man."

In that instant he saw his own despair mirrored in his mother's dark eyes and he tried to take back his words.

"At least Mother, we do know that the 'Emperor of Monticello' loved you. Or , if not that, he desired you, at any rate."

Sally Hemings turned away from her son and back to the window. His hands opened wide in an apologetic gesture and he spoke with a combination of sorrow and bitterness.

"Excuse me, Mother, for speaking so plainly, but I am ample living proof of that man's desire, not to mention my five brothers and sisters as well."

"Seven," she murmured.

"What?"

"Oh, nothing, Madison. Let us put all that aside. When can we prepare for a trip to the old homeplace?"

"Whenever you say, Mother. Let's get the curricle out and we'll go tomorrow if you really are determined to make the pilgramage."

"I am." She turned away from him again and traced a pattern on the flawed window glass. "We loved each other, Madison. And he was a great man. A statesman. Your father was world renowned."

"Mama, we've been over that whole old story hundreds of times." He tried to swallow his bitterness at her usual defense. She can't change now, he reminded himself, she'd invested her life in loving the man. She really couldn't change now. "Let's not argue."

"This 'same old story' you're talking about was my life, young man, and yours!"

"I've said I would take you now." He smoothed the silky curls of salt and pepper hair back from her brow.

"I'll tell Eston to ready himself and on the morrow, Dashing Sally will once again see Monticello in the company of her two sons. I'm just afraid that the trip will make you sorrowful rather than happy."

THE FIRST PART of the trip over the rutted dirt road took only two hours. Silent, the woman and the two young men mentally marked off the miles as they passed the familiar landmarks. To Madison Hemings the heat that rose from the dry grass carried a pleasant fragrance almost like the faintly scented warmth that rises from newly pressed linen. He glanced at his mother from time to time but she always presented a bland face of unexcited acceptance. When they'd reached the boundaries of Snowden plantation, Madison stopped the horses in the shade of a huge elm. He stepped down, then extended his hand to his mother to help her down to stand at the roadside. Eston Hemings stood in the curricle holding the basket of food Sally had prepared for their lunch.

"Jefferson's Country," she announced.

Madison nodded.

"You know they still call it that, my sons. This is still Jefferson's Country."

"Yes, Mother, we know. There's no way to escape the old man, is there? Might as well face up to it." He grinned up at his brother.

"You're both free men because of him."

"You're right. And we're both living because of him."

For a moment mother and son glared at each other, then Sally tipped her head to one side and took a step toward her son. Madison stepped toward his mother. Sally smiled up through her lashes at her next-to-youngest. He smiled back and the two embraced.

"And glad I am that you are living, my son. Both my sons. Come Eston. Shall we eat now?" She smoothed the dark blue silk of her wide collared, high waisted dress.

Madison shook his head with admiration.

"Mama, you're still a flirt and a charmer." He looked up at his brother who nodded agreement. "You could get around any man, even now. Look at you. You're still beautiful."

"True," the younger brother agreed, "That blue silk always makes you look like a woman of quality."

She smoothed the dress again. "My dress and this black poke bonnet were the last gifts your father gave me. A bit out of fashion now, but still serviceable since I shortened the skirt to ankle length."

"You look wonderful and always fashionable, of course, with the shorter skirt. But it's not the dress and it's not the hat. I said *you* were beautiful."

"Only to my sons, I'm sure. Come, come, Eston. Open the back of the curricle. We'll use it as a table."

"Well, Mama, you and Madison can stand around and be genteel, and think white, and talk about clothes or argue over the old man, or even be nostalgic about the good old days if you want to," Eston busied himself at the back of the vehicle then vaulted over the side to stand grinning at his mother and his older brother. "As for me I'm electing to be black and western."

Sally put her lace mitted hand flat against the chest of her youngest as if to read the meaning of his words through his embroidered gray satin waistcoat.

"What are you telling us, son?"

"I'm getting married, Mother. To Jane. We're going to Ohio where we can get free land."

"But son, she's..."

"Yes, Mother. She's black, Mother. Black and free, Mother. Two things I'm sorry to say, we never were in the Hemings family."

"I was only going to say she was...uneducated. Does it not bother you that she speaks the language so badly?"

"Not at all, mama. When I'm with her I'm 'a gonna talk like the rest of them folk'...just as she does. And on a farm out in Ohio I'll certainly not have any use for perfect English nor French speaking nor any other of your fanciful notions."

Sally staggered slightly as if his words had thrown her off balance. "Then I suppose you'll give up wearing your father's fancy waistcoats?"

Without waiting for his answer she turned to stare into the face of her older son as if to learn the truth from him.

"Did you know about this, Madison?"

"Yes, Mama. I knew."

She turned her gaze back to the younger.

"Are you sure this way of life is what you would choose for yourself, son? You're free now, too, you know. You have your papers. You can do whatever you want to do."

"I'm sure, Mama. Jane doesn't mind about my looks."

"I should certainly hope not. Jane is quite lucky. You are a very handsome man." She glanced again at her older son. "Both of you. I know you don't want to hear it but you both resemble..."

"If you think freckled white skin and red hair is handsome," Eston's interruption came muffled from around a mouth full of buttery corn dodger.

"Don't talk with your mouth full, son." The motherly reminder came automatically.

Both Madison and Eston laughed.

"Mama, I can't help laughing. I just told you I was getting married. That I was marrying black, uneducated Jane. That I love her. That I don't want to hear about who my father was. All that should tell you something. I guess you'll just have to finally give up on making me into a gentleman."

"I certainly will never give up on that. But yes. You're right. From now on I mustn't correct you. I must allow Jane that prerogative."

After another hour of lurching over the winding trail they could look upward toward the brick mansion. Their angle of travel gave the three visitors a clear view of the face of the beautifully sited house. Although the plantation had obviously not received the attention of an army of caretakers as it had during their time of residence, the building was still impressive to the approaching family.

Graceful, the pedimented portico still eyecatching, the entire facade was perfectly balanced. Built of red brick finished with white trim, the whole structure sat waiting like a colorful jewel set out upon the lush green velvet of a Virginia summer.

"One hundred thousand bricks," Sally began the chant and, as she continued, Madison and Eston chimed in, "Fourteen pairs of sash windows from London, sent ready made and glazed, along with spare glass for mending."

All three laughed.

"My God, how many times have I heard him say that?" Madison clucked at the horses. "And always just as we approached the house. Always about here."

"He was so proud, Madison. He loved this place better than he..." She let her words trail away.

Eston finished the sentence for her. "...better than he loved anything or anybody in the world."

The closer they came to the house the easier it became to pick out all the points of neglect.

"Every window in the place needs washing."

"Lucky we aren't still living here, Eston. Today we'd be washing windows, brother."

"Among other things."

The horses slowed to an ambling walk and the curricle rolled onto the grass grown drive as Madison guided the animals toward the northern wing, then across the back and into the area between the north and south wings where they stopped.

All three sat silently looking at the house and the encircling outbuildings. The memory-crowded emptiness of the courtyard pressed against them to keep their bodies still and unmoving as their eyes swiftly roved the entire area.

A certain restlessness in the horses seemed to waken the three of them to where they were. Madison clucked reassurance to the two animals, his voice hushed. "We were a part of history, Mother. Maybe someday I'm going to write a book about our lives here." He smiled across at his mother. "Old Juno and Pearl are like me. They must be seeing ghosts."

"As do I, brother."

"And I, my sons."

The brothers helped their mother climb from the chaise, then as if by unspoken agreement, each walked toward a different point, each in silence.

Sally Hemings stood at the top level of the eastern portal and stared first at the door, then she spun slowly in place to look at every part of the inner facade of the plantation's living and working complex. She nodded, then she forced her vision out toward the crumbling slave cabins.

"I remember now just when he first became important to my life." She spoke aloud but the sound was barely above a whisper and her words carried a tinge of surprise. "It was because he wouldn't look at me and it was on the very day she died."

Chapter Two

September 1782

NINE YEAR OLD Sally Hemings sidled up close to her mother who half sat, half lay, in an exhausted sprawl across a wooden backed bench in the corner of the crowded bedroom. Sally put her head against the woman's shoulder and took a deep breath of the wood smoke, warm flesh and lye soap. For Sally, those three aromas always blended with an undentified deeper note to make up the special "mother smell" of Betty Hemings.

"What you doing here, child?" The question was a harsh whisper.

Sally let her muffled answer drift upward from the spot where her ivory skinned face pressed against the gray homespun of her mother's dress.

"I'm hungry, mama."

Betty Hemings' muscular left arm snaked around the torso of her daughter to pull the child close for a moment, then she forced Sally to stand away from her side. With one dark hand she shook the little girl slightly to catch her attention.

"Sh-h-h. Can't you see the Mistress dying?"

Sally turned her huge brown eyes toward the high bed built into one wall of the room. A heavy sweetish smell masked with lavender, wafted from that side of the room. She couldn't see Mistress Martha Jefferson in the bed but she well knew that the sickly woman lay there; had been there, off and on, so long as Sally could remember. The big master sat at the bedside, one freckled arm extended across the bed.

Mrs. Carr, the master's sister, leaned against the linen covered pillows at the head of the bed. Betsy Brown, Critta, Nance and Ursala stood in a group at the foot, their young brown faces mournful. Sally's oldest sister, Betsy Brown, was dry eyed but her next older sister, thirteen year old Critta, wiped at her eyes with the corner of her not very clean apron.

"Critta's crying, Mama." Sally looked back at her mother to see that tears were also making wet trails down her mother's light brown cheeks. Her mother only nodded and repeated the words she had used before.

"Sh-h-h, child. Mistress Martha dying."

From the bed the thin voice of the white mistress rose, entreating the white master and the gathered slave women to care for her children. Sally turned her full attention to the words.

"Our Martha, our Patsy, she is such a solemn little lady. So responsible. You will keep her by you always, Thomas? Critta, you play with her, hear? All of you must take care of our Patsy."

The big red haired man murmured something that Sally couldn't hear. Critta took the apron away from her face to nod assent.

"And Polly, Tom, our Polly and the little baby. You must care for all three." Sally watched Critta nod again and again and use the ragged apron to staunch the flow of tears from her eyes. Betsy Brown and the other young slave women swayed and whispered together. Mrs. Carr bent further into the piled and lacey pillows. The voice from the bed quavered against Sally's ears once again.

"Thomas..." A thin white hand rose in the air, three fingers fluttered a signal and the voice seemed to gain strength, "I can die happy if you promise me one thing."

Sally watched Thomas Jefferson lean even further across his wife's bed. The little slave could hear his answer to his wife this time.

"Anything, my love. Do not die, but only tell me what promise you wish to exact..." His voice shook and lowered, "...and I will gladly do as you ask."

The three delicate fingers trembled anguish into the air.

"I am dying, Thomas."

"Say not so, my darling."

"Yes. I am dying. But it is our three children who trouble me...who trouble my heart. I can die happy if you will care for our children."

"Martha, I will guard them with my life, always." The tall man brushed a hand across his eyes. "You know that without asking. Let us not..."

The three fingers motioned the sobbing man closer and the woman's voice interuppted his plea.

"Oh, Thomas, I can die happy if you promise...if you promise to care for the children alone."

"Alone?"

"Promise me, Thomas, that you will never marry again. I cannot die happy should I think that a stepmother would be brought in over our girls. Oh, please promise you will not marry."

Sally stared and swallowed the lump in her throat as she watched the big man take the shaking feminine hand into both of his own large freckled hands.

"You have my promise, my darling. I will never marry again should you be so unkind as to leave me."

Betty Hemings rose from her sprawl and pressed her daughter to move ahead of her to stand with the others at Martha Jefferson's bedside. The touch of her mother's hand lay warm on Sally's back. When she was close to the bed she could see the woman lying there smiling at the man who held her hand. A pulse beat in the pale women's eyelid as her lashes closed to rest upon her cheek. She drew a long breath, then another and the third breath was a dry, gurgling sound.

"OH, LORD. She gone." Sally heard her mother's comment aloud in the air above her head, then quickly, another harsh whisper just at her ear, "You look, my Sally girl. You remember what you sees. She your sister. Half." Sally felt her mother's forefinger make some sort of sign on her forehead.

For a second the mourning tableau seemed frozen in place, then Thomas Jefferson's sister, Mrs. Carr, straightened and took the sobbing man by the arm and led him from the room. Sally looked up into the man's unseeing eyes as he passed.

"Master's crying." she murmured.

Her mother and her sister Betsy Brown and the other slave women began busying themselves with the laying out of the body. Critta made a motion toward Sally, much like the motion she made when she was shooing the chickens out of the big house kitchen. After a glance at her mother's preoccupation Sally wandered from the room, through the parlor, then drifted toward the master's library. The master's special slave, Jupiter, rushed toward the room with a pail of water, his arm draped with torn cloths.

Irresistible curiosity caused Sally to slip around the door frame of the usually forbidden library. What was going on? Why was Jupiter running? Jupiter never ran. Her wide eyed stare roamed the book laden shelves and across the polished hardwood floor to the prostrate man in the wooden chair with the leg bench.

That was the chair he had had Sally's Uncle John build for his writing. The study table that usually straddled the bench was pushed aside and Mrs. Carr pressed a wet cloth to Thomas Jefferson's forehead.

"Oh, God, Jupiter. He's swooned again. Get someone in here to fan him."

"Yes ma'am."

Sally stepped boldly into the entryway.

"I fan, Jupiter."

Jupiter nodded and for the first time in her life Sally found herself in the master's inner sanctum. She was inside his library, the place where few of the children were ever allowed to go. And she was doing something important, something that only her brother James had been allowed to do before. She pulled on the punka strap with a rush of joy. Maybe the master would be able to see her now, see her doing something especially for him.

AT THE JEFFERSON family graveyard Sally stood with the other slave children and their parents. Only her mother had been told to stand close to the newly dug grave. Betty Hemings stood just beside the white folks who had come to the burial. Sally knew that was because Betty Hemings held the hands of the dead woman's two older daughters, Patsy and Polly Jefferson. Baby Lucy lay in the arms of another slave woman, Isabel. The prayer, the Bible readings, the words from the preacher caught in the breeze from the valley and swept up and over the heads of the slave children then back toward the great house.

Sally took a deep breath. She decided that the scent of moist turned soil mingled with the faint lingering odor of lavender smelled of death. Not unpleasant. Just the fragrance of death.

Sally and the others could see the slow movements and the crying faces but they heard nothing as Martha Wayles Skelton Jefferson was lowered into the earth at Monticello.

What was it that her mother had whispered into her ear the day the mistress died? Sally tried to force herself back into that moment but there was nothing. Only her mother's throaty whisper, "You remember this, girl. You remember this good."

It was a little bit like the lessons, the ones Betty gave her. The spells for using plants and herbs were usually like that. She listened to her mother and she watched and she repeated the strange words but later she could remember nothing, nothing at all. But at the gatherings it all came back. She knew, knew without thinking, knew as if the knowledge came from the bone and blood. She knew what to do.

Her mother had been crying in Mistress Jefferson's bedroom, hadn't she? Had Betty Heming's whispered words really sounded pleased at the gurgling sound of Mistress' death? Sally swirled the skirt of her gray linsey-woolsey dress against her bare leg. Just what was it her mother had said to her...what...exactly?

A twisting pinch in the soft flesh on the back of her arm brought her out of her reverie and she swung at the smirk on her brother James' face. He caught her hand and spoke to her from the corner of his mouth.

"You better behave, Sally. Mama said us be quiet."

July 1784

ON A DAY EARLY in July, coming from delivering the hot cornbread to the workers in the field below the house, Sally stopped to look back westward over the lands of Monticello. She munched on the last cornbread crust she had discovered in the folds of the cotton cloth that lined the basket she carried. The coarse texture of the bread was like gritty sunshine in her mouth. Good. It called for cool water or buttermilk. Something other than thirst stirred within her but she couldn't decide what emotion she was feeling. She knew only that she felt filled with life, heated with the urge to race her imaginary horse toward the western portal of the big house.

"Get up Buceph," she shouted and slapped herself on the buttock as she pranced and arched herself in circles toward the entry drive. "Pay attention, boy, we're going home." She leaped into the air and came down into a steady gallop, her left hand holding invisible reins as well as the empty field basket, her right a make believe whip. She flung her wild mane of glossy dark hair as if truly feeling the sting of the pretend quirt.

The Virginia sun burned through the damp cloak which the July air had earlier wrapped about the plantation and the stones of the road were fire against her bare feet. She jumped to the grass to sooth the pain and her snorted whinneys and animal panting and head tossings soon faded into the heat but her pace never slowed.

"Good boy, Buceph," she praised the horse that only she could see as she reached forward to pat him on the neck, "Settle down, now. We're almost there."

The young slave was unaware of the tall, silent man who stood watching her antics from the window of his study. The solemn gloom of his marblelike visage broke into a small smile. He spoke to the black man who stood arranging books in a large trunk.

"Jupiter, who is the charming youngster just riding her horse up our front drive?"

"A horse, sir?"

"Come and look, Jupiter. I think she will someday be a beauty."

The valet crossed swiftly to the window to stand next to his master and peer down at the now quieting Buceph and rider.

"Ah, yes, one of Betty's sir. Sally Hemings, I believe. She is sister to young James who will accompany us."

"About how old, would you say?"

"She's close to Miss Martha in age, sir. Perhaps one year younger."

"Beautiful." Jefferson murmured. "Betty Hemings...hm...that would make her Martha's half..." He said nothing more but the smile remained as he watched the tiny rider dance against the heat of the portico floor while tying her imaginary horse to the front door handles. He continued to watch until the rider carrying her basket disappeared around the house leaving her invisible "Buceph" tied in the formal entryway.

At the door of the kitchen, under the south terrace, Sally searched through the group of women and adolescent girls who performed various tasks until she spied her mother's gray dress.

"The men say 'Thank you, Betty,' Mama."

"Fine, girl. Here. Run these new ironed linens up to Jupiter. I have all the neckcloths ready in maybe two more hours. You tell."

"Master's white shirts?"

"That's right. Now you run those long legs of yours right on out of here."

"Are my legs long, mama?"

"Long enough. You little, but you still mostly leg. You growing...starting at the bottom. Now, scat. Tell him I going to have these others ready in no time. Tell him."

"Tell master?"

Betty Hemings gave the little girl a playful swat on the backside.

"No, silly. Tell Jupiter. He the one doing the packing."

"Is Jupiter going on a trip?"

"You mighty full of questions this morning. Yes, Jupiter going to Paris, France. Your brother James going too, girl. You know that."

"Paris, France?"

"Get on up to the master's study, Sally girl. Scoot." Her mother made a gesture of dismissal and then was caught up in the work of the kitchen once again.

Sally mounted the narrow stair, tongue between her teeth, concentrating on keeping the neatly folded bundles of white linen safely within her hands. The scent of newly ironed linen roused something pleasurable within her. The exotic words, "Paris, France, Paris, France," made a song inside her head and she mouthed the words silently as she climbed.

She didn't see the taller frecklefaced girl who barred her way until she was almost upon her.

"Where you going, Sally?"

"To take these shirts for Master."

"Give them to me. I'll do it."

"You get out of my way, Patsy. My mama say give these to Jupiter."

"Your mother said to give them to Jupiter," the older girl corrected.

Sally stared at Patsy Jefferson, despair wringing the very depths of her. Even her way of talking, her words, branded her as a lesser person than the other girl. "Said to give to Jupiter," she repeated woodenly.

"You call me 'Miss Patsy' now. Or 'Miss Martha' if you wish. I'm the woman of the house, my father says. I'll take those." She reached for the bundle that Sally carried clutched to her chest.

Sally swiveled to hold the folded linens out of reach. She felt a crumb of cornmeal roll across her tongue. She swallowed and chose her words with care in order to avoid another correction.

"Listen, Patsy, I can't play right now. My mother say...said, I got to get these new ironed shirts to Jupiter. I'll be right back and we can go ride our horses. I just tied old Buceph at the front door."

"I'm not playing. Give me those shirts."

"I'll take them on up and I'll be right back. Promise. Bet my Buceph can beat your Lord William."

The taller girl's freckled face twisted with disdain.

"I said I wasn't playing and I meant it. Do you think I'm a child? I've just come from two years studying with Mrs. Hopkins in Philadelphia. I can speak French, play the harpsichord and, of course, read very well." She sniffed as if the very idea of running like a horse smelled nasty indeed, "As for your imaginary horse...well..."

"How about your imaginary horse, Miss High and Mighty? I seem to remember you been riding Lord William a lot these last few days. Right next to me and old Buceph. As for reading...huh...I can read as good as you."

"Don't you talk to me that way."

"Well then, Patsy, get on out of my way and quit being such a ...such a...dunderhead."

"My real name is Martha Jefferson and you're nothing but a little slave and I'll thank you to remember that. Anyway, you're a year younger than I am and you have to do what I want." The taller girl again reached for the shirts.

Patsy Jefferson paused and stared down at her. Sally realized that somehow, Patsy had sensed that the face below her had changed from being that of just her playmate, Sally. The dark anger that radiated upward toward her had obviously startled the taller girl and caused her to step back.

Sally felt a quick rush of pleasure at her sense of secret power.

At that instant she leaped boldly around Martha Jefferson and when she was on the riser above the one where Martha stood, Sally turned a scathing look into the other's pale eyes. Martha quailed visibly under Sally's hard brown stare.

"I was just playing, Sally."

"No you weren't, Patsy. Philadelphia has made you into a plain old pain. But I'm willing to forgive and forget about it if you are." Sally drillled her gaze into her long time playmate's face for another silent moment. "What you say about that?"

She watched Martha Jefferson swallow and nod before she answered."I didn't mean anything, Sally. Really. I'll wait for you here and we'll go outside, all right?"

Sally nodded and turned to climb to the landing where she again turned and looked down at her master's oldest daughter.

"Go get Lord William saddled up. I'll be down in two shakes of a lamb's tail." For a second Sally watched the other girl smile and clatter down the stairs before she continued upward with her burden. Nausea and rage clambered inside her as she walked. Maybe it would be like last year and Master Jefferson and Martha would only stay in Philadelphia for a few days and then Master Jefferson would turn around and come home...and leave old "Miss Martha-Patsy" back in Philadelphia. Sally grinned at the thought. Martha had hated being in Philadelphia. Hated the school, hated the teacher, hated the other girls. They'd discussed despicable Philadelphia all summer long while on their pretend-pony rides.

Two years before, the Master had been upset that he had not been able to go to France but she had heard him tell her mother that he was actually glad to be back home, to be back at his beloved Monticello. For good, he had said, and now here he was again, going to Philadelphia to take a ship for Paris. Paris, France.

A FEW DAYS later twelve year old Martha Jefferson bent to put her cheek against Sally Heming's face.

"You're my best friend in the world, Sally. I'm never going to forget you. I'll write to Auntie Eppes and ask her to give you my letters." Martha touched her new bonnet. "Maybe Father will buy you a new hat and let me bring it back from Paris when we come."

Eleven year old Sally suddenly became uncomfortably aware of her dirty bare feet and her faded linsey woolsey shift. She stood looking up at the taller girl and something seemed to tighten inside Sally's chest. Martha's red plumed white strawchip bonnet worn over a delicate lace and gauze cap seemed the prettiest hat she'd ever seen. Martha's dimity and lace dress was, absolutely without a doubt, the most stylish frock ever.

She felt the familiar frustration and anger rising inside her. Why should Martha have these things while she was given only cast offs or the plantation made linsey-woolseys? Martha wasn't even pretty. Sally's mother said Martha just looked too much like a smaller version of her father. Thomas Jefferson was a handsome man, or so Sally's mother said, but Martha was thought to be "plain."

Although the time seemed far into the future, Sally was sure that she herself would one day be a woman. A beautiful woman. She had heard the plantation men, both black and white, talk about her looks. Sometimes their comments scared her. Sometimes their words excited her. Mostly the things they said didn't really seem to be about how she looked.

Even so, a beautiful slave wearing rags was nobody. She smoothed her hand against the worn softness of her dress. She wore nothing beneath the shift and she could feel the line of her body through the cloth. Might as well be plain...or even ugly. She felt her sorrow and anger harden into resolution. Somehow, someday, she, Sally Hemings, would wear beautiful gowns and delicate caps and live in a beautiful house. And she'd be free. No one would ever again be able to tell her what to do nor where to go. Someday. Somehow.

"Goodbye, Miss Martha."

"Oh, Sally, I'm sorry." The older girl's mouth drooped. Her voice trembled, "I didn't really mean it. You don't have to call me 'Miss' Martha. Call me Patsy. You're my only friend." She gestured toward her waiting father, "I've got to go with him now but his appointment as Minister will be over and we'll be back in two years, Father says."

Sally felt torn between a bittersweet acceptance of Martha's apologetic farewell and the furiously hollow feeling of being left behind and forgotten.

She watched Martha step up onto the little set of stairs that had been pulled down from the carriage. Martha waved to the crowd and looked wistfully down at Sally. "I wish you were going with us."

"We must go, daughter." The masculine voice caused both girls to turn their gaze toward the tall, broad shouldered man who stood waiting. Sally memorized his appearance in a long glance. His form fitting silver buttoned tail coat was a dark shade of blue. He wore lighter blue trousers buttoned below the knee. Fine dove gray silk stockings outlined his strong, shapely lower legs. His black shoes sported silver buckles and because of their stacked heels he stood well above even the tallest slave who had come to bid him farewell. Sally realized that this was the first time she had ever seen him wearing any footwear other than his riding boots or his carpet slippers.

Martha nodded and held onto her new bonnet with one hand as she made her way into the vehicle. Sally could see tears in the other girl's pale eyes.

At the steps the master removed his dove gray hat and his clubbed, unpowdered hair glinted red fire in the July sun. With the broad brimmed hat he made a gesture of farewell to his gathered household, then stepped into the loaded carriage after his daughter. At the last moment it seemed that his pale glance flew toward Sally and Sally alone. He nodded slightly and he was gone. As he disappeared from their sight the cries and shouts of the plantation's slaves rose in volume.

"The master leaving us."

"What we gonna do? He gone, gone."

"Gone across the sea."

Sally's own mother stood where she had been talking with Jupiter while they waited for the master and his daughter. Fourteen year old Critta moved to stand by Betty Hemings and each cried on the other's shoulder.

Sally ran a few steps after the carriage, then she smiled and waved

and sent an arrow of secret resolve after the receding vehicle.
Someday I'll go to Paris, France, too.

Chapter Three

October 1784

"SALLY, I SWEAR. I don't know what to do with you, girl." Her mother stood in the doorway of the library, one hand on the facing, the other clenching the edge of her apron. "You know you not supposed to be up here. Every time I need you I can't find you because you just hidden away here 'mongst these books. You going to get me into trouble fooling with the Master's belongings."

"I'm not fooling with them, mother. I'm reading them."

"Girl, girl. Reading them. Don't you know you not supposed to do that?" Her mother looked curiously at the rows of books. "Wish you'd put as much study into the charms as you do into this dead stuff." Betty Hemings ran one hand along a shelf. "I guess you can't help it. You too smart. That's why you the one rather than Critta."

Sally kept her finger in the leather bound volume so she wouldn't lose her place. "The one?"

"You know. The one who can take the knowledge."

Sally nodded. Sometimes she wished her mother hadn't chosen her. She walked to stand near Betty to hold the opened book under her mother's eyes.

"See mother. It's a book about Paris, France. This is a map of the city."

Her mother rolled her eyes as if asking for unseen help. "My God, what'm I going to do with such a child? What do I care about a map of Paris, France?"

"Well, you helped me learn to read, mother. You can read too. What's wrong with that?"

Again the mother rolled her eyes and shook her head.

"You not supposed to read, Sally girl. I learned because John Wayles wanted me to learn. But it's against the law, girl. You can get whipped for it."

"You think Mr. Jefferson going to..." she corrected herself, "...is going to whip me?"

"Master not going to whip you but someone might. He not the only master in the world. You almost a woman, now. You thirteen years old. When I was your age..."

"Why did John Wayles want you to read, mamma?"

"John Wayles your... He want me to read because..." Betty Hemings stood without speaking for a moment, a baffled expression on her face.

"What, mother? "

"Never you mind. We got real problems here now.   Word come Baby Lucy and Little Polly was real sick with whooping cough. Polly getting well now, but Baby...she dead." She looked at the shelves of books. "Master going to be sorely troubled. Maybe he be coming home pretty soon. You better see everything to order in here."

The baby dead? Patsy's baby sister? Like all the babies who'd died in the quarters in the last few weeks? Sadness for all the babies' deaths filled her. Her grief for the dead children crystalized her own desire to live. Really live.

Sally again felt the clutch inside her. Was it fear or longing she was feeling? She was growing up and the big man had looked at her. At her alone. She felt the last look from the pale eyes dazzle her again for a moment. As she closed the book and replaced it on the shelf she took a deep breath of the richness of the leather bindings. Life was happening too fast. She realized that she needed time to think, to dream, to plan.

"I'll quit reading and come down and help you get things ready, mamma."

As the days, weeks, months passed it became clear that the master and his oldest daughter were not coming home. Not for another two years, at least. Occasionally Patsy's aunt, Mistress Elizabeth Eppes, came to give directions to the farm boss and sometimes to Betty. Each time Mistress Eppes arrived at Monticello the household rose from lassitude into swirling activity. Everything in the house was cleaned and rearranged.

When she'd gone from the place everyone soon fell back into the easy, indolent happiness of a richly tropical village. Even in cold weather the plantation's pace was relaxed. Laughter came often. Not everything was clean but everyone did what was necessary for the good of the life of the occupants of what was, in essence, a village. Monticello. The little mountain.

Many nights after washing herself all over, Sally would, at Betty Hemings behest, stand beside her mother, both dressed in clean white

linen dresses, while the others danced and sang and writhed about them.
The coarsely woven cloth has been starched and ironed by Sally's
mother and as she danced it was as if her body could feel each linen
thread. Always her nipples angrily withstood the cloth that rubbed
against them. After the ceremony she liked to put her cool hands against
the live fire of her heated breasts.

Sally tried to learn now. She wanted to learn what her mother and
her grandmother had to pass on to her. Gradually she became aware that
the times with her mother were also teaching her what it was to be a
woman.

Sometimes she felt as if she were some sort of gathering machine,
as if she could do the daytime chores, read, write, learn the old ways
and still find plenty of time to do the secret dreaming and planning. It
was as if the languorous ache in the budding mounds on her chest were
throbbing and drumming her an inward message..." Do everything. Feel
everything. Be everything."

At other times she felt almost like the porcelain figurine on the
Master's mantel, unable to move, wrapped in a mantle of longing, but
what she longed for she could not put into words.

Her soul steeped itself in the electricity of the leisurely charged
atmosphere. She felt herself growing and changing. Sometimes at night
there was such pain in her legs that her mother came to her mattress to
rub them, then to sit on them until Sally went to sleep. Her mother
could always make the new stretchings all right, the pained limbs
comfortable.

Sometimes Sally dreamed of pale eyes watching her.

Chapter 4

"STAND STILL, girl, else you going to be wearing nothing but your old shift to Paris, France."

Sally could feel her mother's hands upon her as Betty draped the dark gray woolen cloth against her back. Estelle, the plantation seamstress marked the curving lines with tailor's chalk.

"Can I have a hat, mamma? A new hat? A lady's hat?"

"Girl, you lucky just to get to go on this trip. I can't make you no promises about no hat. You probably wear a headrag." Betty watched the older woman's careful measuring for a moment then looked back up at her daughter. Her eyes held a question. Sally stared back and they came to a silent understanding. "I be asking Mistress Eppes, girl. That the best I can do."

Sally nodded.

Maybe I can make myself a hat, Sally thought, something grown up. A cap and a hat. The hat with a plume. She jiggled with impatience, ready to dart away to try her hand at hat making.

"Girl. I ain't going to tell you again. You gotta be still so Estelle can get your mark for your traveling clothes. Only a few more weeks 'fore we have to have everything all made up for you."

Mentally, Sally thumbed through her new wardrobe. She felt the corners of her mouth turn up with the happiness that the thought of the new clothes gave her. The muslin dress with the watteau overdress for everyday and the blue striped silk watteau sacque dress over the black satin quilted petticoat for best. Sally loved the way Estelle had looped the striped silk back into a panier effect with the black satin roses. "In the French manner," Sally whispered, quoting Mistress Eppes.

She looked down at the worn linsey woolsey covering her breasts. Betty had insisted on the fichu. The ends of the white gauze handkerchief were to be tucked into the bodice at the low cut neck of the blue silk but Sally smiled. She could discard the neckcover as soon as she was out of her mother's reach.

By rescuing two of the late Mistress Jefferson's older dresses, Estelle had cut and reworked a black satin dress into the quilted petticoat and a blue silk dress into the overdress so that the faded patch down the bodice hardly showed. All the seams were new and strong. The frugal seamstress had had enough leftover material to piece together a little cape and a reticule out of the black satin and the blue striped silk.

But that wasn't all. She was to have a pair of Maria's outgrown black slippers as well as her heavy brown leather shoes. Israel had tooled new heels and soles for both and had burnished the worn leather to look almost new.

She looked at the white linen shifts thrown across the table near the stair. Two new shifts. Made out of newly woven cloth. And Betty had promised to put lace on one and embroidery on the other. Sally crossed her arms across her chest and huggged herself tightly with the joy of it. She was really going to go and the only thing she lacked was a hat. She'd look stylish for the first time in her life. She couldn't restrain a giggle.

"Don't get yourself too puffed up, child. You going to have yourself a handful of trouble with taking care of that Maria." Her mother helped the seamstress spread the dark woolen cloth out for cutting. "No hat going to help you do that."

"I ain't...I'm not afraid, mamma. Polly likes me."

"May be. But Mistress Eppes say they be having a terrified child on their hands whenever she talks about her going on the ship. You ever take care of a terrified, spoiled little white child, girl?"

Sally watched the dark skinned seamstress scissor through the swatches of cloth. The cloth felt scratchy and the cut out pieces seemed all higgeldy piggeldy to the fourteen year old but she made no comment.

A gray traveling costume! Out of new cloth made just last winter! Life was too good. She'd just have to have faith and let Estelle's hands and fingers do their magic and those odd looking bits and pieces would eventually swath her in the latest style. After much discussion they'd all three finally decided upon a picture of a two piece traveling costume from Mistress Eppes French Mantua drawings. The lady in the picture had been wearing a hat. A hat with a plume.

"Mamma, can I have the scraps from the silk and the black satin?"

"What you want that stuff for? Not enough to make nothing out of. Good for quilt blocks maybe."

Estelle grinned widely and pulled the small bits of cloth from a basket set near the table.

"Give them to her Betty. Bet she going to make herself a hat. Ain't that it, girl?"

Sally nodded, snatched the offerings and ran from the room with the precious strips and squares clutched to her bosom. She could hear the older women laughing as she ran.

"Your little Sally, she Mistress Growed up Lady now, for sure."

In the library Sally spread the silk across the polished table surface. She could do it. All she'd need was a foundation to cover with the cloth. And a plume. She'd need a plume.

The cap was no problem. Mistress Martha's dimity and guaze caps were stacked in a wooden box in the big bedroom. She'd borrow just one. Sally shrugged away the anger Mistress would have felt at the intrusion if she had lived...for a second Sally was again in the room of death but she pushed the uneasy thought away.

She slipped the key to the attic from the ring that hung in the keybox designed by Master Jefferson. Maybe there would be something else she could "borrow" up there.

The dark mustiness of the attic seemed much colder than the house. She shivered in her well worn shift.

"I should have put on my dress." She spoke aloud to give herself the courage to poke into the hidden corners of the huge room. Shadows danced against the trembling light of the candlestub she carried. She fingered the tiny bag that hung about her neck, her protection against the bad ones. "Nothing up here but old boxes and barrels." Again she spoke aloud. A soft scraping sound skidded against the darkness. "Just mice." The words were whispered.

She again touched the leather pouch between her breasts and whisper-chanted the sure song against evil. The song would help her gain courage as she searched. Mamma was right. She could take on anybody now. She was ready for anything. She was going to Europe. What was in an old attic that could harm her?

Reassured, she watched the boxes and barrels and packages settle into being ordinary things. The light from her candle brightened. Sally closed her eyes and spoke a line of the "finding" spell, then walked directly to a huge wooden chest set against the north sloped ceiling of the room. She lifted the lid and looked down at the folded garments that lay there.

"Master's old clothes."

She took out a small, light gray satin waistcoat embroidered with white geometric symbols. She held the vest to her shoulders then shrugged it on over her shift.

"From when he was a boy, likely."

Digging through the rest of the stored cloth and the folded clothing she felt something hard. Something crushed at the bottom of the chest. She drew it up toward the light. A hat. A sweatstained tricorn felt hat now smashed beyond use for any man or boy. Lifting the hat to her nose she imagined she could sniff the faint odor of her Master's youthful sweatiness. She dropped the lid of the chest and walked swiftly to the lighted rectangle of the door to the stairwell.

She held the battered felt trophy toward the daylight on the stairway.

"I can use this," she crooned, "I can surely use this."

Sally's nimble fingers kept pace with those of the older Estelle. As the seamstress made structure out of a chaos of cloth in the downstairs kitchen, so did Sally pull and cut and steam the old felt upstairs in the library. She saved the discarded pieces of felt and she touched each snip to her lips before she put it into a tiny black satin drawstring bag she'd made for them.

When she was sure she'd found the shape that dipped most elegantly over her left eye she began the final covering with the silk and satin. Piece by piece, she neatly made the tiny, intricate stitches which covered and molded and held the shape she wanted. The desired plume was never far from her thoughts.

On the day that Estelle and Betty brought the nearly finished travel costume for the final fitting, Sally had just tacked the rolled right brim of her hat into place, ready for the plume.

She slipped into the skirt then brought out the altered, fitted waistcoat to cover her old shift. The unlined woolen pelisse strutted a tiny peplum but the rough seams in the cloth no longer scratched her ivory skin. The silk of the waistcoat protected her.

The two older women laughed and commented as they dressed her. It was as if she were their lifelike doll. Before she went to look in the mirror, Sally turned away from them, pinned her dark silky hair up in back then lifted the nearly finished hat from its secret place behind the history books on the shelf. She tipped it forward over her left eye and turned slowly to look at the two women. They fell silent and stared at her as if at a stranger.

"Oh, my God," Betty whispered, "My little girl's a woman."

For the first time in her life Sally heard herself called "Dashing."

Estelle repeated the words she'd just spoken, "She's Mistress

Dashing Sally, now, Betty. Sure enough."

At the services that night Sally concentrated on the plume. She danced for the people and for the Gods and for herself and inwardly she prayed for a plume for her new hat.

THE NEXT MORNING'S sun tried to burn through the fog that lay close to the ground. Monticello's slaves scurried about their tasks with sleep hungry eyes. The Eppes carriage had rolled up the entry drive long before any of the previous night's celebrants were ready to open themselves up to the day.

Elizabeth Eppes stepped inside the cook house building only seconds after Betty Heming had dashed into the room. Betty gave only a moment's thought to her youngest daughter who lay sleeping in their cabin in the quarters. She shrugged into her apron and turned to face the white interloper with a request for a plume.

"A plume? For a hat? My Lord, Betty, I don't even have a plume for my own head." Mistress Eppes stared at her brother-in-law's housekeeper. "Does the child think she's touring Europe? She's only going to take care of Polly. My God!"

Betty Heming nodded understanding. "Girl getting above herself, likely."

Elizabeth Eppes tapped her fingers against the wood of the kitchen table. A small worry crease marred the smooth white skin between her brows. She gazed with unseeing eyes about the brick walled room. Her frown deepened.

"Betty, I'm worried about our Polly. She is never, never, never going to get on that ship voluntarily. What can we do?" The woman's ringed fingers again drummed against the scrubbed wood of the worktable. "And this Sally girl of yours. She's nothing but a child herself." She paced to the wall and back, then to the wall again. She turned and stared back at Betty.

"What does she plan to wear? She can't go around in a shift."

"You remember, mistress, Estelle make her the travel dress with a pelisse. Like your picture show it, ma'am."

"Hmm." Elizabeth Eppes grimaced. "I suppose she'll have to have something else." She sighed and lifted a ring of keys from her belt. "We'll get something from the storeroom. She'll need something to wear for everyday. We'll cut into that new bolt of linsey woolsey and..." she frowned again. "I guess... well, she will be Maria's maid, after all...and in Europe...Betty, I suppose you should cut off enough linen to make her two aprons and a cap while we're in there." She trilled a nervous laugh. "The French are so...strange. About slaves, you know. Our Polly musn't be shamed."

When the two women returned to the kitchen building with the yards of gray linsey woolesy and the white linen cloth, Mistress Eppes reminded Sally's mother again.

"Something plain now, Betty. You hear?"

"Yes'm."

"She can have pockets, I suppose, but mind you, no fancy petticoats."

"Yes'm"

Elizabeth Eppes let the coarse linsey woolsey slip from her arms onto the scrubbed tabletop. She stared at the puddle of cloth but it was as if she didn't see it.

"If Sally can get Maria onto that ship without her crying you can tell her I'll get something for her hat. Something. Maybe not a plume," She stepped closer to Betty, "But something. Something nice." She walked the circuit of the room again. "I'm just worried sick."

Betty nodded.

"We think of something, Mistress. Sally, she's a pretty smart young girl child."

"I'll go then." Mistress Eppes allowed a glint of gratitude to flash toward Betty Heming then she flounced from the building and whirled toward her carriage.

Betty and all of the other slaves looked at the back of the Eppes carriage as it rolled down the hill. Most watched with undisguised relief. Many fell down just in the spot where they'd been working to try to catch up with their lost hours of sleep.

Sally stumbled into the kitchen building only moments after Mistress Eppes' departure.

"Critta say you want me, mama?"

"You better wake up girl and get your mind to work." Betty plunged one of her hands into a deep wooden batter bowl. With the other she poured milk into the dry mix, then began kneading the ingredients.

"I'm still sleepy, mama."

"Well, wake up Sally. Wake up, now. Your time about to come." Betty squeezed the white biscuit mixture through her hands then lifted one batter covered finger to point at Sally, "And you going to have to pay for that hat."

Chapter 5

Spring 1787

GULLS SWOOPED overhead, their cries wild and exotic in Sally's ears. The sights and sounds and smells of the filthy, crowded, Norfolk dock all competed for her attention. The waves lapped against the wooden pilings making the structure seem unstable beneath her feet.

She held the hand of the youngest Jefferson daughter but her eyes and her nose and her ears were making a million discoveries. Already she was a world away from the plantation where she'd lived nearly all her life. Jefferson's Monticello and John Wayles' farm where she'd been born. That was all. Those were the only two places she'd ever known and now, now she was on her way to France.

"Come on up, Polly," Jack, the oldest of the Eppes Children leaned over the rail of the small ship. "We're playing hide-and-go-seek. I'm it." He gestured to the little girl who held onto Sally with one hand and clutched at her aunt's skirts with the other. "I'm it. I'll let you in free if you'll come and play."

"You want to play with Jack and the others don't you, darling?" Elizabeth Eppes looked over the head of her niece and into the young slave's eyes. "Sally will play, too, won't you Sally?"

"What? Oh, yes ma'am." Sally nodded. She felt the black ribbon cockade on her handmade hat flap juantily in the Virginia Breeze. "Come on, Mistress Polly."

"Are you going on the boat, too, Aunt?" Eight-year-old Polly kept her hold on Elizabeth Eppes' skirt.

"Of course. Your Uncle Frances and I will be right behind you." She nodded at Sally. "You two girls run on and join the game. We must talk with Captain Ramsey." She bent to embrace the child. "Before you go up give Uncle and Aunt Eppes a kiss, Maria."

"Come on you two!" Jack's urgent call bounced down from the rail. "Everybody's already hiding."

Maria Jefferson pulled away from her aunt's embrace. The child tugged Sally toward the gangplank.

"Hurry, Sally."

Sally skipped to keep up with her new charge. She felt the carefully tipped new hat shift on her curls. She'd piled her dark hair to spill out the front of her new linen cap. Now the hat was slipping away from the lace edged cap. The yards of cloth in her new woolen skirts swayed and momentarily caught in the spaces between the bars of the guardrail.

"Come on, Sally. Jack's waiting."

Sally glanced back at the Eppes who were just stepping onto the walkway. She felt a quick moment of sympathy for the twisting grief on the face of the older woman.

"She really don't...doesn't want to lose the child." Sally told herself but she had no time for sympathy because Polly had dropped her hand and was running ahead across the deck of the vessel. "You done started your job right now, girl." She spoke to herself as she entered into the noisy game with the other children. Soon the grownup hat and the stylish pelisse were laid aside in the heat of the game.

Later, below deck, she lured the smaller girl into the cabin that would be theirs. "This would be a good place to hide."

"Look, Sally. One little bed on top of the other." Maria seemed enchanted with the tiny cabin they were to share.

Sally smoothed the mahoganey bulkhead paneling with one hand. She couldn't help sharing the smaller girl's enthusiasm. The cabin seemed cozy, even luxurious, the round window just right for the tiny space.

Elizabeth Eppes peered over Sally's shoulder into the cabin.

"Want to climb up into the top bed, darling? It's called a bunk, I believe."

She squeezed herself around Sally to lift the child to the top bunk. Maria stretched to touch the ceiling of the room.

"Look Aunt, I can touch the ceiling just sitting here."

"Yes, dear." Mistress Eppes turned to smile at Sally. "This is a wonderful place to hide from the others, Sally. I'm glad you found it."

Sally smiled but said nothing. The hours of play had prepared her charge for a nap. While the child slept the family could leave the ship. The ship could cut loose from the moorings and Maria would awaken on the Atlantic. Her carefully worked out plan seemed to be working.

"All right Polly, you lie down in that bed and I'll get in this one down here. They'll never find us here."

Maria clapped with excitement then flattened herself onto the top bunk. Elizabeth Eppes stepped toward the passageway and the child sat up and wailed her displeasure.

"What is it, dear? You want to play, don't you? You don't expect me to stay and play with you children, surely?"

"Yes," Polly's lower lip poked forward. "Yes, I do. I want you to stay."

"Oh, very well. I'll just sit on the edge of Sally's hiding place until one of the boys finds us."

Sally lay on her back, the cotton wadding mattress smooth against her shoulders. Mistress Eppes' dark skirt filled her vision but Sally wasn't seeing the woman. She closed her eyes. She could smell old sweat and powdery sachet and the scent of oiled wood. This was certainly different than the shuck pallet on the floor of her mother's one-room cabin.

She opened her eyes and closed them again. The gentle rocking motion lulled her into that space just between sleeping and waking. Behind her lids she could see herself strolling along the deck of the ship, dignity and adulthood regained. The pelisse and the hat made her look like a woman grown. "A growed-up lady," they'd called her at home. In a moment the same picture began but with imagined Paris streets rather than the ship's deck as her background. She slid into sleep.

A harsh gloved hand covered her mouth. Sally's eyes flashed open to see that Mistress Eppes stared down at her, a finger across her lips. With her head she indicated the upper bunk then withdrew her hand from Sally's face.

"She's asleep," the woman mouthed the words, "We're going."

The mistress stood and Sally swung her feet noiselessly to the floor.

"Tell her we love her. Take care of her." The whisper was followed by the quiet closing of the door.

She was alone with the child. The family was leaving. She and Polly were on their way to London, then Paris. Paris, France. Master Jefferson knew they were coming. He'd be there to meet them. Mistress Eppes had explained everything. What would he think of her? Would he see she was a woman now? All dressed up. "Dashing," the folks at Monticello called her.

She glanced at the sleeping child in the top bunk then eased herself back onto the lower bunk and allowed herself to slip back into her daydream. Now, in the dream, a tall red headed man walked the

Paris streets by her side.

"AUNT EPPES! Jack! Auntie!" For a moment Sally couldn't understand where she was. The cries came from above her, the screams now mingled with strangled sobs.

She sat up and her forehead crashed against the wooden frame of the bunk.

"Oh-h-h-h, God." She staggered to stand. She put one hand over the blossoming goose egg above her left eye. She steadied herself with the other hand.

"Polly. Sh-h-h-h. I'm here. Don't cry. Everything's all right."

"I want my Aunt Eppes." Polly Jefferson's face screwed into a red mask of fury. "I want Jack. I want to go home."

"We're on the ship, Polly. Remember? With Captain Ramsey? You liked him, didn't you?" Sally rubbed the bump again. If the silly child would only quit screaming maybe they could see the ship, meet people, find out about the other passengers on board. After all, Captain Ramsey had said they were to come to the bridge whenever they wanted.

"Let's go see what Captain Ramsey is doing." Sally reached to lift Polly down. Polly slapped at Sally's hand and screamed more loudly. Her feet flailed an angry rythmn into the bunk's thin mattress.

"Go home...I want to go home."

Sally lifted the kicking, screaming child and set her on the floor. Polly dashed toward the door and out. Before Sally could grab the hat and her pelisse, Polly disappeared into the darkness of the passageway.

Sally raced to catch up with her. At the bottom of the ladder near the end of their passageway she could not see the child so she began her climb to alert Captain Ramsey.

On the bridge where one of the ship's sailors stood at the wheel, Sally could see Polly snuggled against the Captain's shoulder. He was pointing out to sea as if he were explaining where they were going.

Sally slipped forward to stand silently behind the two.

"Aye, Miss Polly me girl, you're a very good sailor, I see. You and I are going to have a great and wonderful trip to England, now aren't we?"

Sally watched the child's head nod against the Captain's chest.

Captain Ramsey turned to Sally. He frowned.

"Young woman, are ye not supposed to look after this wee one?"

Sally nodded.

"Then see ye do that, girl." His frown turned to a smile which he directed at the younger girl as he released her to stand in front of him. "Miss Polly here is signing on as my first mate. See you have her up here on the job at first light. Mind now." His countenance again turned solemn. "You," he pointed his chin toward Sally, "You have a sacred duty, now, girl. See you tend it."

Sally took Polly's hand into her own. "Yes sir."

"That's 'Aye aye, Captain,' me girl." he again smiled down at Polly. "Kin you say that, wee one?"

Polly giggled.

"Aye aye, Captain."

Sally's, "Aye aye, Captain," was a whispered echo.

Chapter 6

SALLY BRACED herself against the bow railing and took deep breaths of the moist air. She strained to see what lay ahead. Huge waves lifted the ship then dropped it into a watery trough, only to lift it and drop it again. She saw nothing but gray water disappearing into a veil of gray fog. Every day of the four weeks they'd been on board she'd stolen a few minutes to come to the very front of the ship to peer into the mist or the fog to see if she could see England. The constant spray had made her hair, her cap and her apron stiff with salt. Still, she could not resist the urge to keep searching for the land.

"No use looking, me girl. We won't be sighting land for yet another week."

Sally whirled to watch Captain Ramsey amble by pulling Maria on the small wheeled cart they kept on deck. The little girl wore the Captain's cap and stood against the front rail of the cart guiding her "ship" from her imaginery wheelhouse. The Captain sent a fond glance back at the tiny sailor.

"And even then Miss Polly may make land afore ye. She's still me first mate but she's also been made captain of her own ship now, ye know."

"Come on board, Sally. Ride on my ship." Maria's shout was a jubilant command. "We're on our way to England."

A quick glance at the Captain's face assured her that whatever Polly wanted was what he too wanted, so she waited until the ship settled for a moment then she lifted the linsey woolsey skirt of her new everyday dress to step onto the child's "ship."

"On to England," Maria ordered the Captain and he smilingly resumed his circling of the cleared deck area.

Sally noted the surreptitious glances of the sailors as they went about their duties with ropes and pails. Her cheeks warmed but she kept her glance lowered as the Captain had insisted she do from their first night on board.

"A looker like you, me girl, could cause a riot on me ship. You'll nay be staring bold at the lads, now girl. Doest hear me?"

Sally had nodded, half thrilled, half shamed at the idea of causing a riot by merely looking at "the lads."

The Captain had complained several times about the Eppes sending their niece in her care. He had mumbled "young beauty" as if he were spitting out a dire epithet.

But so far the trip hadn't been all bad. Neither she nor Polly had been sick. Little Polly could always make the dour Scot smile, even laugh. She was free to run and play and talk with the crew, all of whom seemed to adore the child almost as much as did their Captain.

Sally had to admit that Polly was a charming child. More fun perhaps than her big sister, Patsy. Prettier too, by far, but inwardly Sally thought of what an adventure it would have been if she'd had her old tall, plain faced, Patsy on the boat with her. She and Patsy could always talk together and Patsy had always let Sally lead her. With little Maria she had to be the "adult," the one who looked out for the other child. She had to play childish games with her. "Her duty" she told herself whenever she resented having to be "it" yet once again in some game.

Sometimes Sally felt a touch of envy at the other youngster's freedom to do exactly as she pleased but the envy could usually be banished by the vision of herself, dressed in her grown up new dress which she hadn't yet worn. She'd be walking down a Paris boulevard. Most often, in her vision of the future, a tall man strolled by her side. He doffed his hat to passersby, but his real attention always centered upon the "young beauty" Sally Heming. After all, Polly Jefferson was just a child, an infant, really. And she was grown up, now.

"Here, girl. Get my first mate down to her cabin and to her dinner now." The Captain's booming voice tore the fabric of Sally's dream and Maria's deckbound "ship" came to a grinding halt. Polly jumped up and down to be carried belowdecks and Captain Ramsey obliged by lifting her high in the air then depositing the eight year old in Sally's arms. "A special treat for you today, mate. But you mind Sally now, and you eat your meat and potatoes first before you have it."

"What is it?" Polly was laughing and calling over Sally's shoulder now, "What's my treat?"

"I'll nay tell ye, child. It will be on Sally's tray until you've well and truly finished your other victuals." He moved toward the ladder laughing with pleasure.

In their passageway, Sally put the child down so she could run ahead to their cabin. From the food odors Sally realized that Polly was having roast beef and gravy again. She hoped they'd put some of the gravy on her potatoes as they'd done last time. The cabin boy stood just to the left of their door, their tray held on one of his hands, shifting easily with the ship's movements in order to balance his load. To Sally he looked like a man but she knew he wasn't very old because the Captain and all the men called him "Boy-o." He was taller than Sally and had a soft, blond down on his face that showed he hadn't yet started shaving. He wore a ragged jersey but he always looked clean, as though he washed himself and his clothes, often.

Sally wished there were a way she could wash. The years of bathing before ceremonies had developed that odd need in her. She loved the feel of her body and hair when they were clean. She knew it was silly but she longed for a chance to soap herself all over, to immerse herself in warm water and simply let herself drift in the luxury of it. Maria had screamed so loudly their first night on board when she'd tried to wash the child's face that she'd settled for a quick wipe of the girl's mouth and hands after each meal.

Boyo brought them nearly a half pitcher of water each day but Sally knew she dared not use it for washing herself. Water on a ship was for drinking and for making tea. Nothing else. The Captain had made that clear. She couldn't waste it on herself.

"Brought your vittles." Boyo's voice had almost finished changing. Sally didn't look at him but she nodded and went into the cabin to seat herself next to Polly on the lower bunk.

"Captain say, Miss Polly don't get her treat until she done et the rest of her food."

Through her lashes Sally could see the look of hunger that the young man cast toward the two plates of food on their tray. "Maybe some white children hungry, too." she told herself with a touch of surprise. It was such a novel idea that Sally tucked it away in her consciousness to examine at a later time.

"Thank you, Boyo. I'll see to it." Sally indicated the space on her bed where he usually placed their food. "We'll be finished in a little while."

Polly was already holding her golden prize in the air and shouting. "It's just like Christmas. I got an orange. I got an orange."

Sally stared with wonder at the shining globe in the child's hand. She felt Boyo do the same as he left the room. "Peel it for me, Sally. I'm going to eat my orange, first."

Sally followed Polly's directions for peeling the fruit and she put the discarded peelings on the corner of the tray nearest herself. Polly grabbed the fruit and climbed to the top bunk with her treasure.

"Your meat...and your potatoes...and your hardtack, Miss Polly. The Captain said..."

"I don't want any of that old stuff. You eat mine, Sally." The room was filled with the tropical fragrance now. The child sucked contentedly on section after section of the fruit.

Sally scooped the meat from Polly's plate onto her own. She paused, then she cut the slice of beef in half and placed the slightly larger piece back on Polly's plate. She also placed half of the thick orange peel on the child's plate and kept half for herself.

When Boyo came for the tray, Polly was drifting into sleep. Sally pointed to Polly's uneaten portion and indicated to the cabin boy that he was to eat what was there.

After a quick glance at the sleepy child overhead he scooped up the potatoes and meat and finished them off with a couple of bites. He sniffed the orange peeling, then placed it carefully into the piece of cloth he wore to hold up his faded trousers. He held the hardtack biscuit in his mouth as he backed his way out of the cabin. Sally thought she could see a message of thanks in the nod he gave her before he closed the door.

When he'd gone, she put her half of the greenish orange peeling into the pocket of her dress and then she lay back on the cotton mattress to nibble on her own circle of hardtack. The distant creaking of the ropes and the groans of protesting wood were unnoticed background music for the dream that she was surrounded by all the glorious perfumes of the East Indies.

Chapter 7

THE ANCHORED ship's deck felt strange beneath Sally's hard earned sea legs. She wondered if she could even walk on the land. Excitement at the closeness of the busy London docks forced her to breathe deeply to preserve her calm. The breaths brought the reality of the docking. The busiest harbor in the world smelled of dead fish and garbage and human waste.

She gazed across the rail, over the short stretch of dirty water, to see the teeming life of the docks. Straining porters, well dressed women, foreign sailors and a thousand other people and happenings she couldn't yet comprehend, seemed to call to her.

"I ain't going." Polly Jefferson clung to the roped rail. "I'm going to stay with Captain." She turned her tearstained face up to the bearded man. "I can stay with you, can't I? I'm your first mate, ain't I, Captain."

Sally moved to take the child into her arms but Polly screamed and clutched at Captain Ramsey's legs.

The Scotsman's face betrayed his anxiety. For long moments he looked into Sally's eyes as if he were sending her a message. What could they do? What could she do? They'd just have to take the child off the ship whether she cried or not. Sally caught her lower lip in her teeth. What a disappointment. She'd have a loud and squirming child to control while she wore her silk dress for the first time. She glanced again at the swarming dock. She felt such longing to step into that crowd, to become a part of it. She sighed and shrugged.

"I'll take her, Captain Ramsey, sir."

The Captain shook his head almost imperceptibly.

"No, not now, Sally me girl. Leave us not be hasty, now. Why don't ye and Miss Polly here just go on back down to your cabin for a wee while?" He put his hand on Polly's head. "I'll come by and get the both of you when my duties allow. In the meantime I'll send Boy-o with some tea for you two fine young ladies." He lifted Polly's chin with the back of his hand, "Will ye keep some tea for me, then, little one?"

Polly nodded and hiccoughed.

"Go on with ye, then," He looked at Sally, "You stay alert, me girl." He raised his eyebrows as if he'd just realized something. "When I've offloaded mayhaps we can all three go to have a look at England. Do ye ken?"

Sally nodded her understanding and sighed again as she turned to steer the younger girl toward the cabin they'd shared for five weeks.

Polly chattered happily all the way to the room below deck.

Sally felt frustration rising within her. "Why does he want to wait?" she fumed inwardly, "It'll just be the same, whether we go now or two hours later. Even if we wait until tomorrow she'll likely scream and kick."

Inside the cabin she lifted her hat to place it on the end of her bunk. She gave the black ribbon cockade a fleeting touch before she rose to answer Boy-o's knock. Polly stood on the edge of Sally's bunk and held onto the lower rail of the upper bunk. She bounced her glee at the arrival of the young sailor.

"Here's Boy-o. With tea." She jumped to the floor then jumped back up onto the rail and hung there, swinging one arm in the air.

"Captain told me to bring you ladies tea."

"Thank you, Boy-o." Sally looked at the steam rising from the large pot in the center of the tray. "Why don't you get another mug so as you can have a cup with us?"

"Yay!" Polly's excitement rose a notch. "Have tea with us."

Boy-o returned to their cabin in minutes. He put his hand into the cloth band at his waist and smiled sheepishly.

"Filched some biscuits," he mumbled. "One for each of us and two for Miss Polly."

Polly's shriek of delight caused the older youngsters to smile at each other.

Boy-o stood leaning against the mahogoney paneling to drink his tea and eat his biscuit. Polly sat near Sally's hat and kicked her heels against the lower wall of the bunk to show her contentment. Sally huddled against the small pillow at the other end of the berth. For a moment each of the three kept silent, the creaking of the wooden timbers the only sound. The cabin boy looked at Sally with his usual searching interest. He opened his mouth, then closed it.

"Did you want to ask me something, Boy-o?"

"Uh...no, uh, no ma'am." He looked away.

"Don't call me ma'am, Boy-o. I ain't...I mean, I'm not a ma'am. I reckon you can just call me Sally."

The boy stared again.

"Are you really a slave, Sally? The men say you're one for life?"

Sally looked down into her mug of tea.

"Yes. For life."

"I thought all slaves was black. I ain't never seen any slaves 'cept was black men. You look white to me. And you a girl."

"My skin is light but Miss Polly is my mistress."

"Yes," Polly crowed, "I'm her mistress."

The two adolescents ignored her shout.

"And you're so beautiful. Dressed like a lady."

Sally felt her cheeks warm. She looked again into her tea.

"Thank you. The Mistress back home, she tell me she want me to look respectable for the sake of the family."

"Family?"

"We the Jefferson family, from Monticello."

"Oh," Sally could tell he was still puzzled.

"I'm Polly Maria Jefferson," Polly was now walking the lower bunk rail holding onto the upper rail. Boyo backed into the doorway. "Polly Maria Jefferson!" She chanted the words, "Polly Maria Jefferson."

"I got to go, Sally. We're taking on cargo. Shipping out in three days time. Back to Norfolk." He smiled at Polly, "You want to sail back with us, Miss Polly Maria Jefferson?"

Sally raised her hand as if to stop his words but it was too late.

"Yes, yes. Back to Aunt Eppes. I want to go! And Sally will go too." Polly slapped the top mattress for emphasis.

Sally could read Boy-o's alarm at Polly's reaction and at her own gesture of warning. He ducked his head, mumbled good bye, scooted back into the passageway and disappeared.

Polly jumped down to follow but Sally held her by the skirt.

"Let me go, Sally."

"You don't want to go now, Polly. Remember? We have to wait for Captain Ramsey." She gently trolled the little girl back toward the bunks, "Don't you want to wait for the Captain?"

"Oh, all right. I'll finish my biscuit." The child flopped back onto the bunk and held out her mug, "More tea, Sally."

Sally stood to pour the dark liquid. It felt strange to pour tea without having to brace herself against the bunks.

Both girls froze at sounds on the other side of the door, sounds of a voice talking and laughing with the Captain, a woman's voice. The two girls looked at each other in shock. They were supposed to be the only females on Captain John Ramsey's ship.

Chapter 8

"HERE, GIRLS. Come and meet a fine lady and her husband." Captain Ramsay knelt to lift Polly against his chest, "See here, Miss Polly...I want ye to meet some friends of mine, friends of your father," He smiled at the wide eyed child, then at the well dressed woman standing just inside the door of their stateroom.Got two plumes in her hat, I see. Sally peered from beneath lowered lashes to note the torrents of snowy lace that rippled from the collar and sleeves of the woman's rich, purple velvet costume.

"This here is Maria Jefferson, Mistress Adams," John Ramsay lifted Polly a bit higher so she was eye- to-eye with the older woman, "Polly, this be Mr. and Mrs. Adams."

Polly turned her face and mumbled into the Captain's chest, "Sod the bloody woman," then burst into tears.

"Polly!" Ramsay and Sally remonstrated in unison.

The child cried even louder.

"My apologies, ma'am," Captain Ramsay pushed his hat toward the back of his head then lowered his hand to scrape his fingers through the auburn curls of his beard, "Methinks the wee one has been associating too much with rough sailors."

Sally surreptiously stared at the astounded woman and her husband. She had a hazy recollection of seeing the couple at Monticello. Neither the woman nor the man had yet spoken a word.

"Now ain't ye sorry to speak so, me girl?" He shook the crying child slightly, "And these be your old daddy's friends."

Polly gulped back a sob and looked at Abigail Adams. "Where is the old bloke?"

Sally gasped but Mrs. Adams acted as if "old bloke" were a normal and acceptable way to ask for one's father.

"Oh, darling, he's coming from Paris. Mr. Adams and I..." She pulled the little, black garbed man forward, "Are going to take you to the embassy to wait until Mr. Jefferson arrives from Paris."

The woman's words made Sally's heart sink. Not here? The

Master not here?

Polly flung her arms around the Captain's neck and clutched him tightly in her determination to stay with him. Her wails echoed through the ship's passageways.

"Child, child. You're choking the old Captain. Come now." He pried her arms from his neck and placed her on the floor. She raced to Sally and buried her face in Sally's skirt.

Poor little child, Sally thought. She's here because he want her to come and now he's not here. She looked down at the heaving shoulders. Probably getting snot all over my new dress. But Sally didn't move.

"This is Sally. She is Miss Polly's...sl...uh, servant."

The middle-aged woman looked Sally up and down and then once again.

"This young woman accompanied Jefferson's daughter across the ocean? What can he be thinking of?" Mrs Adams turned to her husband. "Can you believe that Elizabeth Eppes allowed the child to wander around the world with a creature like this?"

The small man surveyed Sally, mumbled "humpf" then backed into the corridor, "Step outside, dear," he ordered, "You too, Captain, if you please."

The three adults huddled just outside the door. Polly again buried her wet face in the silk of Sally's skirt. Sally stood with one hand on the smaller girl's shoulder. She didn't look at the three conferees but she strained to hear their every word.

"...ship her right back to Virginia." That was the woman.

"Exactly." The little man.

"I have to agree, ma'am. She can go right back with us. Never should such a one have been sent with the little Miss." Old traitor. And she'd thought the Captain liked her. What did he mean calling her "such a one?" Through the silk of her dress Sally touched the small bag that hung between her breasts. Maybe time to use some of the learnings.

She tightened her hold on Polly's shaking shoulder. She felt like echoing the smaller girl's muffled sobs.

"I will not leave now," she promised herself and Sally, "I won't go back with his ship."

Polly nodded understanding into the blue striped silk. Her sobs quieted to an occasional sniff. She looked up at Sally. "If you go with that old woman Sally, I'm going too. Stupid old cow."

"You better quit that there sailor talk, Missy." Sally smiled down at the tearstained face, "You're going to get yourself, and me, into a peck of trouble."

Polly swung herself onto the bottom bunk. "Well, I'm not going anywhere. Not without you, Sally." She kicked the wooden rail. "And where's my dodrotted father?"

Sally settled onto the bunk bed beside Polly. She kept her attention on the three in the passageway as she lifted the small black satin bag from inside her dress. She smoothed the tiny fetish within both palms and closed her eyes.

"What you doing?" Polly peered at the movement of Sally's hands.

Sally didn't answer.

"You better answer me, girl. You want me to have you tied to the mast and whipped with the cat-o'-nine- tails?"

"Just a juju bag."

"Juju? You're doing voodoo, Sally? Aunt Eppes will be really perturbed with you. She says that's the devil's work."

Sally kept her eyes closed but she broke her concentration long enough to murmur, "Hush, Polly."

"You trying to keep from going back to Virginia?"

Sally nodded but continued her inner chant and the movement of her hands. The silky bag began to feel uncomfortably warm but she maintained the rubbing motion. A slightly sweet fragrance seemed to emanate from her palms, overpowering the room's normally damp and moldy odor.

"Put me in, too, girl. You hear?"

Sally smiled and nodded again.

The buzz of talk from the hall rose in volume.

"Well, it's decided then. We'll take both Maria and the slave girl. Maybe that's best for now."

Sally could hear the relief in the Captain's reply.

"Oh, ma'am, that really may be the best way. Our Miss Maria Jefferson has a mighty strong disposition. Mayhap she'll go along easier if you take pretty Sally, too."

"We will keep a sharp eye out for the littlest Jefferson." John Adams turned his head to look in at the two girls, "And I suppose we must keep the mulatto by us, at least for the time being."

"You are still American Ambassador to the Court of Saint James, sir?" Captain Ramsay asked.

"We are," Mrs. Adams answered, "And a filthy lot of back stabbers they are. They wouldn't think of speaking to a 'colonist,' much less to a 'colonist's' wife. I, for one, am ready to go home."

John Adams gave a short barking laugh.

"The women are snubbing Mrs.Adams, Captain."

"Their loss, ma'am."

Captain Ramsay being gallant, Sally thought. She touched the heated bag to Polly's shoulder then to the area of her own groin.

"That's hot, Sally."

"I know. You wanted to be in it."

"Touch me again, girl."

Sally laughed. "No need. We going to be all right. We going... we're going to see your papa soon."

"I ain't going to no dodrotted Court of Saint James. Not without you and the Captain."

"Oh, Polly. You got to clean up your mouth. Me too. You really might get me whipped it you keep up with that sort of talk. We're with the Englishers now."

"I ain't no Englisher."

"You're a little girl and you're going to be seeing a lot of important people, Englishers or not." Sally tapped Polly again, then whispered, "I want you to help me and I'll help you. Will you do it?"

Polly nodded solemn agreement, her gaze on Abigail Adams who had again swept into their cabin. The eight year old lifted her arms as if to embrace the woman.

"Is my Aunt Eppes your friend?"

"Oh, you little darling. Indeed she is, and I hope you and I can be fast friends, too." She lifted the child and hugged her close. Polly pulled her face from the white lace frills which threatened to engulf her.

"And Sally, too?"

Mrs. Adams pursed her mouth a bit, then nodded.

"And Sally, too." She looked as if she'd bitten into a persimmon before the first frost.

"And the Captain, too."

"Sure and I'll be along, me girl. You and Sally, here, you go along with Mr. and Mrs. Adams and I'll get me work done on board, then I'll be right along to join ye." He held out his arms. "Come, me sweet. I'll carry ye to the gangplank. What say ye to that, girl? What say ye to that?"

Mr. and Mrs. Adams swept toward the upper deck, Mrs. Adams leading the way. The Captain and his small burden trailed behind the Ambassador. Sally grabbed her hat and brought up the rear.

Over the Captain's shoulder, Polly smiled at Sally and muttered the words, "I say, damn and bloody blast," and she put her hand over her mouth, then giggled.

Sally couldn't help it. She let her own laughter bubble up and spill over her lips. Everything going to be all right.

Chapter 9

"MR. ADAMS, what are we going to do with the child?" Abigail
Adams threw her hands up in the air, "Either she's in tears or she's
acting like a rough little sailor."

The worried woman turned to look at her husband. The ruffles on
her white morning cap seemed to vibrate with frustration.

"She's been with us for two days and, my dear husband, I am at
the end of my tether."

Adams nodded and motioned his wife to join him at the table.

"Perhaps she would like a visit to some function or other, my dear.
Get her mind off her childish troubles."

"Well, I just give up. She clings like a leech to that Sally girl or
she screams for Captain Ramsay," Mrs. Adams clashed her porcelain
teacup into the saucer on the table on front of her, "I could just kill
Thomas for putting us in this position."

"My dear, we did trick her into coming home with us...telling her
the Captain would come soon..." He too put his cup down,"...and now
we must pay for our untruth." He stood and put his napkin beside his
plate, "We would never have done such a thing with our own children,
Mrs. Adams." He bent to kiss his wife's cheek, "I must go, dearest.
You'll just have to cope."

Mrs. Adams sighed and rose to walk to the door with her husband.

"Well, the slave girl is quite a child, but she seems fond of little
Maria."

"And she seems good natured," John Adams bent to peck again at
his wife's cheek before he stepped out the door, "We're going to have
to make the best of things. I rather like the little Jefferson."

Abigail Adams watched until her husband's carriage disappeared
then she mounted the stairs to check on her houseguest.

"Good morning, darling."

"Good morning, Mistress Abigail," Sally spoke for her charge.
Young Polly sat hunched in the window seat, staring out onto the
London street. Sally shrugged and glanced toward Polly. The eight-

year-old begant to half-mutter, half-sing, "Do you ken John Peel at the break of day? Do you ken John Peel? Do you ken John Peel when he's far away? When he's far, far away with his fox and his hounds in the morning?"

"Have you had breakfast, darling?"

"Yes, ma'am. Thank you." Sally again answered for Polly who let the mumbled chantey die to a whisper.

Abigail Adams raised her eyebrows then strode toward the bent figure.

"Well, Miss Maria. How would you like a trip to Sadler's Wells? For the ballet? They say it's fun, very entertaining."

"I had rather see Captain Ramsay for one moment than all the fun in the world," Polly looked up at her hostess, "When will he come?"

Sally watched Abigail Adams seat herself on the window seat and draw Polly Jefferson close.

"Darling, I must tell you the truth." The woman closed her eyes for a moment and took a deep breath, "The Captain is already on his way back home. He won't be coming to our house." She smoothed Polly's disheveled hair back from her face. "I'm sorry, darling."

Sally watched Polly sit in silent shock for a moment then she touched the little girl's shoulder when Polly began to sob quietly.

"SHE BE ALL right, now, ma'am," Sally patted Polly on the head, "I done told her Captain not coming. Now she believes what I said."

For a moment the three females sat in shared silence.

"Your father will be here any day now, Maria, love," Mrs. Adams kissed the child's forehead, "Everything will be all right, then."

"Yes, ma'am," Sally's voice was almost a whisper.

"Yes, ma'am," the little girl's answer echoed Sally's words.

The three spent the day together. A dressmaker measured Polly for a party dress, Abigail and Polly insisted that Sally eat lunch with them in Polly's nursery bedroom, then the three of them took a turn around the graveled paths of a nearby park.

At dinner Ambassador Adams expressed pleasure at his wife's glowing face.

"Your day went well, I see."

"Oh, Mr. Adams. I learned something. The little one's temper and her sensibility are just formed to delight." She sat at her husband's left and placed her napkin on her lap, "I'm becoming very attached to the child...in spite of all her sailor talk." She rang the bell for the maid,

"And her...servant, Sally, she was just a pleasure to have around, too," She looked at the offered dish, sniffed, then nodded approval and waved the server to offer the dish to her husband, "I can't believe that a slave would be so well read and so well spoken." She tasted her wine, "A little schooling and that girl could fit right into London society."

Adams chuckled.

"You're of quite a different mind, tonight, I see."

Abigail Adams nodded.

"I may try to talk Thomas into leaving the child here when he comes. What would you say to that idea, John?"

"Don't plan on such an arrangement, my dear."

"I know. I know. Now, I suppose I'll have trouble giving her... them, up."

Adams shook his head and chuckled again. "Methinks, Mistress Abigail misses her motherly duties."

"I'd enjoy having a daughter for a time, Mr. Adams. That might make our time in this nest of wasps go much more quickly," She took a large helping of kidney pie, "Both girls bring a little touch of home."

Her husband raised a warning finger.

"Her father will come soon, my dear. Enjoy her presence while you can but don't plan on a long visit. Thomas may come tomorrow."

ONE MORNING Sally sat up in her bed and stretched luxuriously. She touched the juju bag and yawned widely. Suddenly a thought flashed through her mind and pierced the last fog of sleep from her. She and Polly had been living in the Adams' house for three weeks.

Three weeks! And Master Thomas Jefferson had not yet appeared.

Chapter 10

"SO...NOW YE won't have long to tarry here, me girl."

Sally paused with the tray the cook had just handed her.

"What do you mean?"

"Did ye nay hear the noises in the night?"

Sally shook her head. She searched the dishes before her to see if the bread pudding Polly had asked for was on the tray.

"Could I have cream for her pudding, please, cook?"

The Adams' cook sniffed and sent an underling for the clotted cream.

"She be a mighty spoiled young lassie, if you ask me. And you Sally, you indulge her entirely too much, young woman."

Sally smiled across the tray and nodded agreement.

"A little discipline would do the child a world of good," The older woman chided Sally with a flour covered finger, "You keep right on letting her have her way and you'll have a young monster on your hands. Mark my words, now."

Sally felt helpless to explain her own special situation in the slave/mistress position to the roly poly, wage earning servant. Better agree and change the subject, she decided.

"You're probably right," Sally kept her voice noncommittal, even in tone, "What were you saying about noises in the night?"

"Ah. Last night it was. Ye didnae hear? No, of course not, you're upstairs w'the lassie," She pointed to the servant's sitting room, "Got us a Frenchie in there. Sleeping on the couch, he is. Your master's servant, they say."

Sally felt her heart clutch in her chest.

"Master Jefferson? He's here?"

"Nay, nay, girl. His servant, I say. Name of Petit," She pounded the bread dough she had rolled out onto the marble pastry board, "Come to fetch you two," She raised her eyes to look into Sally's face, "Has naeone told ye?" She clicked her tongue against her teeth, "Expect not," She hit the dough a hard smack, "Quite strange they be, these colonials," she muttered.

Sally took the proffered cream and hurried to the servants' stairway. She craned to see the stranger but the couch was not within her sight. She wanted to run to the third floor but she didn't dare chance the safety of the china and glass that filled the tray. Her measured tread to the nursery seemed to take forever.

"Polly, Polly. Here's our food. And I have a surprise." Sally let her voice trill the last three words.

"What, what?"

Sally set the heavy tray on the nursery table. She laughed down at the sleepy eyed child.

"Splash some water on your face, Miss, and come to table. Then I'll tell you. Maybe." She laughed again and fanned her face with her apron, "If'n...if you eat your breakfast."

The two girls ate quickly without talking. Polly greedily licked the clotted cream from her spoon. Sally dreamed of being in Paris.

"Well?" Polly broke the quiet.

Sally jerked to attention.

"Well, what?" She grinned at her charge.

"What were you going to tell me?"

"We're going to Paris."

Polly's smile died.

"Is that all? Aw, Sally, I know that." Her word sounded weariness and boredom with the whole idea.

"But, Miss Polly, did you know that your father's servant is here? Right downstairs? Came last night?" She tapped a happy rythmn against her teacup. "His name is Petit. He came for us, Mistress Polly. Now, did you know that?"

Polly's face crumpled. Tears flooded her eyes.

Sally sighed. Another uphill battle. Another scene. This child was the cryingest child in the whole world. Always spoiling the excitement with her long face and her tears. Sally felt a tiny prick of guilt at the thought.

"Now what, Miss Polly?"

"I want to stay with Mrs. Adams. Or go back to Aunt Eppes," She gulped out a sob, "I want to go back to Virginia. I want to go home, you stupid bloody cow."

In the face of the child's sorrow, Sally tried to quell her own rising excitement. Polly really was too young to be shoved from one stranger to another. But what could she do for the little girl? Nothing. And

Paris? The city's name glimmered like a waking dream in Sally's mind.

"Don't you want to see your father?"

"I hate him." Polly raced to throw herself across the still rumpled bed.

The child's unhappiness pulled at Sally for a moment, then the excitement rose again within her.

"We're probably leaving tomorrow, Mistress Maria. Best you make the best of it," Sally picked up the tray, "Come on, child, Paris is a wonderful city," She swept through the nursery door, "They speak French there," And holding the tray high, she galloped two stairs at a time down to the kitchen. At the bottom of the stair she took a deep breath of the midday cookery.

Cabbage. And something she couldn't identify. Smelled good. Sweet. Treacly.

"Cook, when will we be going? Did anyone say?"

"How is your little miss taking the news?" The cook pulled a threaded needle to close the huge bird which lay in a black roasting pan on the table in front of her, "Upset because her father didnae come after?"

"Well, she don't want to leave Miss Abigail. That's for sure." Sally put the used dishes into a pan and filled it with warm water from the well on the side of the kitchen hearth. She rubbed a cloth across a bar of lye soap and began the washing up. "All she wants to do is go back home."

"Can't say I blame the little one. No telling what might be going on over there with those Frenchies." The cook shoved the bird into the huge oven, "I hear her father didnae come because of a woman. A married woman." The cook turned to smile at the young slave, "Same name as the young miss, Maria something or other, they say..."

A hard kernel of despair rose to catch in Sally's throat.

"Someone...named Maria?...He loves her?"

"Don't know about that, girl. He is a man, after all. Feeling his oats, I suppose. I just know that he was expecting his friend Maria in Paris so he sent that Petit to fetch you two youngsters."

"Is he...she's married?"

"So they say."

For Sally the trip back up the steps was an exercise in drudgery. He and a woman. A European woman. Her dreams fled before her. The Master. So in love he would not even come for his beloved youngest daughter. And she? Sally Heming? She was no one and nothing to him.

As she entered the nursery she fell across the bed to let her own sobs mingle with Polly's despondent whimpers.

Late in the afternoon Abigail Adams drifted into the nursery. She carried a sheet of paper in her hand which she handed to Sally. She nodded toward the letter and signaled secrecy with her finger across her lips.

"I was here earlier but you two were asleep. You both looked as though you'd been crying." She held her hands out toward Polly, "Come here, darling."

Polly ran to be clasped in Abigail's arms. Sally wished with all her heart that she could share in that embrace.

Chapter 11

July 10, 1787

MY DEAR THOMAS,

"...upon Petit's arrival Polly was thrown into all her former distresses, and bursting into Tears, told me it would be as hard to leave me as it was her Aunt Epps. She has been so often deceived that she will not quit me a moment least she should be carried away. Though she says she does not remember you, yet she has been taught to consider you with affection and fondness, and depended upon your coming for her, and not have sent a man whom she cannot understand. I express her own words...

I have not the Heart to force her into a Carriage against her will and send her from me almost in a Frenzy, as I know will be the case, unless I can reconcile her to the thoughts of going and I have given her my word that Petit shall stay until I can hear again from you."

Silently, Sally read the copy of the letter which Mrs. Adams had sent to Thomas Jefferson, then the extra page which held the note copied from John Adams' angry postscript;

"...And I am extreamly sorry, that you could not come for your Daughter in Person."

Sally's gaze met Abigail's over the head of the crying child.

"Mr. Adams is quite in a great huff about this whole thing, Polly," she looked down at the child, "And I promise that Mr. Petit shall stay right here with us and so shall you and Sally until we have an answer from your father or he comes to fetch you himself."

"We just wait, ma'am?" Sally could not decide whether the news was good or bad. She'd learned to love Abigail and London was a fine city...but...there was Paris, and there was her brother James Heming, and especially, there was Master Jefferson. All. Still a long distance away.

"There isn't anything else we can do, so let's make the most of the time, shall we?" Abigail Adams stood, and taking Polly by the hand she moved to the window to look out on the busy city street. "We'll take a carriage ride through the park, shall we?" She turned her face toward Sally, "Would you like that?"

"Yes, ma'am. We'd like that, wouldn't we Polly?"

Polly gulped back a last quavering sob and nodded.

"Yes, a carriage ride."

After the ride Mrs. Adams brought the servant Petit to the nursery.

"Maria Jefferson, this is your father's servant, Petit."

Polly held out her hand to the small man.

"How do you do, Mr. Petit?"

"Ah, is Maria, no is Polly?

Mrs. Jefferson explained, "Her name is Maria. She's named after Mr. Jefferson's sister Mary. But we all call her Polly." She kept her hand on Polly's back.

Petit shook his head.

"Pardonez moi, madame, zbeak non English."

Abigail lightly touched Polly's head, "Polly Jefferson." She touched the child's head again, "Also Maria Jefferson...aussi Maria Jefferson."

"Oui," the Frenchman smiled his understanding, "Pollee, et aussi, Maria."

Abigail moved to stand next to Sally.

"This is Sally Heming. Sally is Maria's doyenne."

Sally put her hand in the little man's hand. His palm and his fingers were as soft as a woman's hand, a rich white woman's hand. Petit was no laborer. Abigail... Mrs. Adams, said he was a servant. What kind of servant wore ruffles at his wrist and had no calluses on his hand?

Petit nodded his understanding of Sally's place in the Jefferson household, then he lifted her hand to his face and brushed the back of her hand with his lips.

"Cheri, mon cheri ami, Sallee. Bonjour. Soon, welcome to France." His brown eyes never left her face and when he lowered her hand he held on a moment longer than was necessary. Sally tugged her hand from his and felt her cheeks warming.

"Thank you, Mr. Petit."

Abigail Adams bustled the little man out the door and away from the nursery before the French servant could say another word. She rolled her eyes as if she'd beheld the very thing she'd feared all along. She spoke to Sally over her shoulder. Her words almost a whisper.

"Sally, keep away from this one. I'll explain later."

Polly tugged at Sally's skirt.

"Sally, why can't he speak English?"

"He's French."

"He smelled funny."

"I think he was wearing scent."

"Why did he kiss your hand?"

"I believe that's what Frenchmen do."

"Well, he better not try kissing my hand nor my foot either. I'll kick his bloody ass."

"Polly, for the Lord's sake. you've got to quit talking like that. Mrs. Adams is going to wash your mouth out with that lye soap if you not careful."

"Frenchey better watch out."

"You're the one who'd better watch out. What in the world is Master Jefferson going to say about you, child?"

"He better watch out, too."

Sally sighed and bent over Polly's embroidery hoop to help the child turn a stubborn french knot with pale blue silk thread.

Inwardly she relived the brush of the soft, male lips against her skin, the sound of 'Sallee,' of 'Cheri,' against her ears. The spicy sweetness that rose from the lace at his wrists when he moved his arms. The look in the foreigner's eyes had been admiring, searching, even hungry, and something else she couldn't identify. Sally shivered. She touched the tiny satin bag at her breast. Stay away from him. Yes. She'd do that.

In the three weeks that followed, Sally made it a kind of a game to try to get in and out of the kitchen without being accosted by Mr. Petit. Sometimes she won, sometimes he did. His sly smiles and his French compliments felt greasy against Sally's soul. After a few moments with the Frenchman she often daydreamed of ice gray eyes and pale skin, of tall American bones, and the humor of freckles.

When the letter came telling them to come to France, the trunks and bags and packages were all ready to be shipped. The morning of the beginning of their Channel voyage, the cat and mouse game came to a head. Only she and Polly and Monsieur Petit would be making the trip.

As they drove away from the Adams' house, each of the three celebrated their departure in his or her own way. Inside the rented carriage the Frenchman smiled. Sally looked out the windows at London passing by and Polly wept.

Chapter 12

PETIT STEPPED down from the rented public carriage and reached to help, first, Polly, then Sally to step to the Paris pavement.

Sally stretched and tried to grasp the whole boulevard in one quick glance about her. She filled her lungs with the deep, smokey, perfumed, fresh bread smell of Paris. She had to take Polly's hand to keep her from darting into the way of the wagons, tumbrils, carriages and other horse driven vehicles which rolled a constant thunder across the cobblestoned pavement.

"Careful Polly. We in Paris, now, child. Really in Paris. You stay right here by me. We see your Father in a few minutes, maybe."

The serving man nodded at Polly. "Paree. Polly see Papa."

He then let his gaze wander over Sally's face. A stream of words poured across her ears. The words were liquid, the sound beautiful to her. She shrugged her nonunderstanding but she smiled down at Polly.

"Polly, I think I'm going to try to learn French."

Polly looked up at her and grinned.

"Not me. This bloody Petit fellar jabbers more than the pickaninnies in the quarters. Anyway, who'd want to sound like that?"

Sally lifted her skirt with her other hand and the two followed the still talking Frenchman up a short set of steps and onto a stone landing. He lifted the brass lion's head knocker and the three stood and waited until the heavy door opened. In the doorway, James Heming gasped at his sister.

"Oh, my Lord. Is that you, Sally?"

Sally stepped close and put her hand on her brother's arm. "It's me. And the little one. Are you going to let Miss Polly and me come in?"

"Oh, my Lord. Come in. Stay right here. I'll get Master. He just ready to leaving."

Her brother whirled and raced down the long entry hall. Sally stared at the richly papered upper walls and the wood paneled surround. Overhead a crystal chandelier picked up shards of light from the still opened street door. Petit trotted around the two girls to follow on

James' heels. Sally and the littlest Jefferson stood hand-in-hand, transfixed at the elegance of the Paris townhouse. Silent seconds passed.

"Is this my father's house, Sally?" Polly's words were whispered.

"Yes," Sally moved closer to her charge, "It's prettier than the Adams' I think. Almost as nice as Monticello, ain't it?" She kept her voice to a murmur.

"I don't remember Monticello, you silly cow. Just Aunt Eppes'." The eight year old kicked one of the wooden chairs that flanked a chest against the wall, "It ain't as nice as Aunt Eppes' house."

"Isn't."

"Well, you just said 'ain't.'"

"I'll make a pact with you. I'll remind you to say 'isn't' and you do the same to remind me when I forget. Shall we do that?"

"All right. Is a pact the same as a promise?"

Sally's nod stopped in midair. Both girls turned to look at the man whose tall silhouette moved toward them. James darted around a corner behind his master, then as quickly turned to disappear from their view.

As Jefferson moved into the light from the door the low slanting sunlight showed Sally the man they'd traveled so long and so far to see. She remembered his eyes when he'd looked at her before he and Patsy left. His gray eyes. She was only eleven years old then, but she remembered. And now, here he was, looking at her again. That same kind of silver-eyed survey. She shivered slightly and touched the tiny satin juujuu bag which rested warm between her breasts under the silk of her dress then she pulled Maria Jefferson forward.

"This is your father, child. Greet Master Jefferson, now."

Polly remained silent, her frown deepening. The unsmiling man knelt on the black and white tile floor and held his arms out to his daughter. Polly tried to slip behind Sally's skirt. She shook her head "No" and looked plaintively up at Sally.

"Polly. Go on. Don't be silly."

The man's cool gray stare raised to again entrap Sally's wide-eyed gaze.

"Abigail said you were quite a child, Sally Heming. It is good to see you," He turned his pleading look toward his daughter, "Can we not be friends, my darling daughter? You look so very like your mother." He looked up at Sally again, "And you..." He stopped. "How old are you now, Sally Heming?"

"Nearly fourteen, sire." The sound of the deep masculine voice had made her arms tingle, her belly feel as if it were turning over within her. She remembered that voice.

He nodded and again turned his attention toward his reluctant daughter.

"Can we at least shake hands, Miss Maria?"

Polly nodded from her blue and black striped silken hideaway and put her hand into the large freckled hand. He pulled the child gently toward himself and embraced her loosely with his other arm, as if he felt he must curb his hunger to hold her close.

"Ah, my child. I thought you'd never arrive." His gaze returned to survey Sally. "Perhaps we might talk whilst the little one is resting? Perhaps you can tell me of the gardens and orchards and of the people back on my little mountain? Were the windows shining in the sun? Was all well there when you left?"

Sally nodded.

Thomas Jefferson stood and lifted his daughter to his chest. He gestured to Sally that she was to follow.

"Let's go see your big sister, little one."

"Miss Patsy?" Sally felt a tiny prick of excitement at the idea of seeing her childhood friend, "Miss Patsy's here?"

He glanced over his shoulder. "In this very house. And waiting eagerly for you two."

In the dark paneled, booklined room at the back of the house, a tall, rawboned, young woman stood outlined in a sunny garden window. The figure took an inadvertant step forward when the man and the two girls entered the room. Patsy Jefferson ignored her father who let his younger daughter slide to the floor. Patsy's gray eyes stared at Sally.

"Is that truly you, Sally?" Sally could hear the real sound of welcome in her old friend's voice. Patsy lifted her arms and Sally did the same as she stepped close to accept the embrace of the tall, freckled, young woman.

"It's me, Patsy...Miss Patsy. We done come a long way to see you."

Patsy held onto Sally's shoulders and stepped back. "Look Father. Sally Heming is all grown up. Dressed up. Beautiful. Wearing a hat." She embraced Sally again. "I am so glad to see you. I've been lonely." Her glance at her father carried apology. "Father is always so very busy." The gaze she bent on Sally held their old secret promise to "tell-all-about-it-later...in-private."

The plain faced, auburn-haired girl smiled down at her prettier younger sister. "Aren't you glad they've finally come, Father?" She asked, and knelt to try to hug the frowning Polly.

Thomas Jefferson's deep voiced answer to Patsy's question caused Sally to smile and look very closely at the toes of her new black boots.

"Yes. I am extremely glad to see both our darling little Miss Polly and our own beautiful young Sally Heming." He cleared his throat. "I too, have been lonely."

The moment was swept away in the rush of tears and sobs loosed by Polly.

"Sally, I want to go home. I don't like it here."

Chapter 13

SALLY ROSE and splashed cold water on her face before slipping into her gray everyday dress and her new white linen apron. She spared hardly a glance for the small, almost empty, servant's room. Patsy and Master Jefferson would be down for breakfast soon. "Hurry, hurry." She breathed the words for her own benefit.

When she stepped into Polly's room to waken the youngster she felt her heart melt and she smiled at the sleeping, tear-swollen face.

"Poor little girl," she crooned, "Time for breakfast. Time for your new life." She bounced on the edge of the high bed and surveyed the place. Polly's room was three times the size of her own, the walls papered with a deep green velvet flocked wall covering, green velvet draperies hung at the two windows.

"Come on, girl. I know you're not asleep. Just playing possum. Rise and shine." She looked at the highly polished dark wood chest, table and chairs that stood at the end of the silk canopied bed. "Nice room, Pollykins." She ran her hand down the pink and green striped silk of the bed canopy. "Come on, honey. Try to be happy." She bounced hard on the bed again. "Ain't nothing we can do about it anyway." She glanced at the tightly shut eyes of her little mistress. "You're putting on your act again, Miss Polly," She leaned to pull one of the little girl's blue eyes open, "Yoohoo. I see you in there."

Polly grinned and opened the other eye.

"You said 'ain't.'"

Sally nodded. "You caught me."

"Do we got to stay here?"

"We have to stay here, Polly," Sally gestured at the well-kept room. "You have a beautiful place to live. Your father and your sister love you. I love you." She shoved the covers back and lifted the child to the floor, "Now, we're going to have us a good breakfast."

Polly didn't resist when Sally pulled a dark blue woolen dress over her touseled head, then bent to fasten the child's shoe buckles. She allowed Sally to wipe her face and hands with a damp linen cloth and smooth her hair with a wide toothed comb.

Sally stood back and looked at her handiwork. "You look very nice, Miss Maria. Here," Sally handed a thick envelope to the child, "Give this to your father. Mayhaps he'd like some news from home. Your Aunt Eppes sent it to Abigail's so we could bring it on to Master Jefferson."

"Do we have to stay here?"

Sally nodded. Sally could read the sadness in Polly's eyes. An eight-year-old shouldn't have that pinched look, that look of an old woman, she thought. She pushed Polly ahead of herself into the wide hallway.

"You wait at the table. I'm going to go down and help in the kitchen."

"No."

"Polly...don't be a goose."

"Wherever you go, I go."

"Silly child. Go meet your father."

"No."

Sally shrugged. "Suit yourself. Let's scoot for the kitchen." She strode toward the bowels of the house, to the basement kitchen, with Polly trailing listlessly behind, dull fright written on her face.

In the warm kitchen, Sally and Polly had to stand aside while the French cook and the French maids bustled about with the meal preparation. Petit stood smiling at them from the opposite corner of the smokey room. When the first maid took a tray to carry to the dining room, Sally lifted it from her hands with a whispered, "Merci."

Polly plodded up the steps behind her and in the dining room she stood against the wall near the serving buffet.

"Sit down, Polly."

"No."

Sally again shrugged and continued unloading the dishes of food.

Thomas Jefferson preceded Patsy Jefferson into the room by only seconds. He smiled, helped Patsy to her chair then sat at the head of the table.

"Good morning, darling Polly. Good morning, Patsy," He paused for a second, "Good morning, Sally Heming."

Sally suddenly felt as if her chest were full of feathers. She kept her eyes on the task before her.

"Good morning, Master."

He pushed his chair back and pulled another chair out from the table.

"Come Polly. Come sit here."

"No."

"Now Polly, do what your Father say."

"No."

"What's wrong with the child, Sally?" His eyes mirrored his puzzlement.

"She just scared. We come a long way. We saw a lot of people. Now she's maybe homesick."

Patsy rose and moved toward the buffet.

"Oh, so am I, little sister." She turned to smile at her father, "Father misses Monticello, dreadfully, don't you, Father?"

"I don't miss Monticello," Polly muttered.

"She misses her Aunt Eppes, likely," Sally explained, She placed the teapot at Jefferson's right hand.

"All right, Polly. We understand," the gray eyes seemed to burn an icy trail on the back of Sally's hands as she poured his tea into a large cup, "Now, come and sit here by me."

"No."

"Young lady, march yourself to this table and sit down." The male voice rumbled thunder in the room. The gray eyes flashed lightning. "We don't need this on your first day at home."

"Not my home."

Sally stood behind Polly and braved the icy gray look.

"Let her be with me today, sire. She'll be all right. She just grieving right now."

His glance seemed to cool even more and his lips thinned.

"Maria Jefferson. Sit down." He rose to his full height, his voice crashed against the walls, "Sit down here."

Polly shook her head "no."

"Not unless Sally sits with me."

"Sally?" His voice betrayed shock, his eyes sought Patsy's, "Sally?" Patsy nodded. He returned the nod.

"Of course. Sally Heming, won't you join us at breakfast table?"

"Oh, Master Jefferson. I couldn't..."

"Aw, come on, Sally." Polly pushed her to sit on the chair Jefferson had pulled out. Sally understood that was so she would be between the father and daughter. She smiled reassurance toward Polly.

Sally settled herself and Patsy lifted the table bell to call a maid from the kitchen.

"It seems my daughters both think a great deal of you, Sally."

"I love them, too, sire."

Breakfast passed silently. Sally stole small glances at each of the Jeffersons as they ate. Whites were always quiet when they ate. Not like in the quarters. A good meal was always like a celebration. Jefferson broke into her musing when he rose to leave the table. As he stood he nodded at Sally.

"I expect we'll see you at the supper table, Sally Heming," and he left the room.

Sally felt a shock of pleasure. Was she not to be a servant, a slave? What exactly was her new role to be int his family?

Patsy giggled and reached to touch Sally's fingers.

"Let's spend the whole day gabbling, Sally. Papa seems to like you. We'll catch up with everything and let the French servants take care of the work."

"Yeah," the younger sister chimed in, "Let's gabble all day. Let the Frenchies do the work. Bloody bastards."

Patsy uttered a shocked "Polly" and covered her mouth with her hand.

"She just mimicing the sailors from the ship, Miss Patsy. Pay her no mind. She's trying to shock you. She knows better."

"Oh, Sally. Call me Patsy...when it's just us. I suppose, in front of others, you'll have to say, 'Miss Patsy' but when we're alone or with family...it's Patsy."

"Yeah. Old Patsy. And call me Polly."

Sally felt a tingling in the center of her forehead, as if a tiny door were opening there. Life was changing. Maybe too fast.

"Oh, Patsy. And Polly. I'd like that."

"And you're going everywhere I go, right Sally?" Polly swung Sally's hand in her own. "And I want you to sleep in my room."

Sally nodded. "We'll see what the Master says." She thought she'd just been elevated to a new position. Now, all she had to do was learn what that new position might be.

Chapter 14

"I FORGOT THE blasted letter!" Polly slid from her chair and raced from the room, "Mr. Jefferson," she called, "Mr. Jefferson. I have a letter for you."

"Mr. Jefferson?" The tone of Patsy's voice asked Sally for an explanation. "She calls him Mr. Jefferson?"

"She don't know her father, Patsy. She hasn't seen him since youall left two years, nearly three years ago." Sally stood to begin clearing the table, "She been living with your Aunt since your mama died. That's a long time, girl." She swept table crumbs into a napkin, "She didn't even know me when we started out from home. Life ain't been easy for your little sister these last few months."

Patsy stood also. She put out a hand to stop Sally's work. "Sally, just quit that. Let the maids do it." She put her hand through Sally's arm, "Let's go upstairs to my room so you can tell me everything."

The returning child crashed into the two at the door of the dining room. Knocked askew, Patsy sprawled on her seat in the doorway, Sally fell to her knees in the hall. Polly leaned against the door facing and laughed boistrously.

The two older girls looked at each other as if to say "One must excuse a child" and Sally smiled. "I guess she found Mr. Jefferson."

Polly nodded. "He looked at the package, Sally...but he didn't open it."

As Sally stood she explained to Patsy, "Your Uncle and Aunt Eppes sent a letter to your father at the Adams House and since he didn't come to England to pick us up, Miss Abigail asked us to bring it on to Mr. Jefferson." She dusted her gray skirt where her knees had landed on the floor, "That would get it to him faster than posting it, they thought."

Patsy remained seated in the doorway. She looked at the floor for a moment before she lifted her eyes to stare into the space above Sally's head.

"You all want to know why he didn't come to England?"

Both Sally and Polly nodded.

"I want to know everything about the Master," Sally admitted silently.

"It was that old Maria. Maria Cosway. He was waiting for her." Patsy pulled herself up and stood brushing the seat of her fussy white lace and cambric dress. "She was supposed to come to Paris." The next words came tumbling out, "With her husband." She cut her gaze toward Polly. "They're European friends of our papa. They live in Switzerland, I think...and I don't like them much." She turned her look to Sally and nodded as if to say, "There's more to this than I'm telling."

Maria Cosway? Had she heard something about the woman at the Adams House? Sally tried hard to dredge up the memory. The name sounded familiar. Almost like an echo in her head she could hear Abigail's voice speaking, "He's seeing that Maria Cosway again." and John Adams' dry answer, "Not our business, Mrs. Adams."

The pieces of the puzzle fit. They had been talking about Master Jefferson...and a woman named Maria Cosway.

"I'll get the whole story out of Patsy," Sally promised herself as the three girls headed toward Patsy's bedroom.

In the large room, paneled much like Polly's bedroom, the draperies and bed curtains were of dark pink satin. In the space in front of the windows stood a full length mirror. For the first time in her life Sally looked at herself from her head to her feet. Well formed breasts, tiny waist. She looked into huge brown eyes, saw a mop of deep brown curls. Sally could now see what others noted when they looked at her.

"If I were as beautiful as you, Sally, I could find a rich husband right away," Patsy came to stand behind her, her red head above Sally's dark curls. She smiled at their image and Sally smiled also. "I'm still so much taller than you, Sally."

"I guess I won't get much taller," Sally heard the tinge of apology in her own words and she looked at Patsy to see if she had hurt her friend's feelings. Being short was so much better for a woman. She watched Patsy stretch a hand up into the air well above Sally's head.

"Can you believe I'm still growing? I'll be up to here in the next year. I love my papa but I wish I took after the Wayles like Polly and you, rather than after papa and the Jeffersons."

"Sally and me take after the Wayles?"

Sally shook her head at Patsy and gave their old index-finger-on-the-chin-just-below-the-lip silence signal. Maybe the Master wouldn't like them talking about his dead wife nor about Master John Wayles, either.

Patsy nodded understanding and moved quickly onto another subject. "Maria, did you like the room I chose for you? I remembered that you used to like green. I've always wanted to wear pink and Father won't let me so I chose the pink room."

"I like it well enough." Polly bounced on the edge of Patsy's bed. "Anyway, my bed's softer and Sally is going to sleep in my room."

"I'm so glad you're here." Patsy bent to put her arm around her little sister. "I've missed you. You've turned out to be so pretty."

As the two sisters chatted, Sally tested the daybed and each of the chairs. Most held cushions upholstered with a cheerful rose printed chintz. She drifted about to quietly explore every inch of the room. In the corner nearest the bed she sniffed a slightly acrid odor. Curiosity caused her to lift the square cushion that rested on the seat of the tall wooden armchair. Under the cushion was a hinged wooden seat which lifted. Under that was another wooden seat which had a round cut-out in the center. Through the cut-out she could see a rose trimmed chamber pot which rested in the cubicle below.

Patsy grinned and came to pull open the hinged bottom front of the chair. She removed the china utensil and held it high in the air.

"Pretty fancy, isn't it? I just throw off the cushion, lift the seat and sit on the chair whenever I want to relieve myself. The girl comes in and takes the pot away twice a day to empty it and clean it." With a grin she tossed the rose covered bowl to Sally, "It's so convenient. You don't even have to leave your room to pee. We need to get some of these at Monticello. I'll bet papa will see to it when we get back."

"Yes, I expect he will," Sally caught the newly washed, heavy white bowl by the handle and spoke the rest of her answer inside her own head, "And I'll probably be the one who gets to do all the washing out of the dratted things."

After Polly was sent to get more white linen and colored floss from the housekeeper, Sally looked expectantly at Patsy. "About Maria Cosway?" was what she hoped her look said to the older girl.

Patsy seemed just as eager to get the story out in the open. "He's been seeing this woman ever since we got over here. Her husband doesn't seem to notice...or maybe he doesn't mind." She picked up her embroidery hoops and flopped down on the daybed, "Sometimes they go on trips together...Papa and Madame Cosway...just the two of them." Patsy punched her needle angrily through the linen, "She writes to him." She raised her pale eyes to lock onto Sally's brown gaze, "Don't tell, but I've been afraid he was going to marry her...even if he did promise Mama that he'd never remarry."

"Didn't you say she was married?"

"Yes. To an ugly old man. A European. They move from husband to husband or wife to wife over here, Sally. The men aren't like our men back in Albermarle County." She gave the linen another vicious punch. "She makes me sick."

At that moment Polly skidded back into the room with a wad of wrinkled linen under her arm, colored thread trailing behind her, Patsy busied herself sorting the silken thread and smoothing the cloth.

"Men aren't so very different in Virginia," Sally spoke the words inwardly as she moved to help Patsy untangle Polly's mess.

"How many dresses did you bring, Sally?" Patsy looked intently at the gray linsey woolsey that Sally had felt so proud of earlier.

"This one and the silk dress you saw yesterday and a heavier woolen one I wore on the ship."

"That's all?"

Sally nodded but didn't speak. What could she say? She'd been so proud of her new clothes but maybe there was something wrong with them?

Patsy hung her head to ask the next question.

"Could I try on your hat? The one you wore yesterday? It was so stylish."

"Sure, Patsy," Sally smiled at the taller girl, "I'll go get it."

When she returned with her pride and joy, Patsy lifted it to her red curls and tried to place it at the same angle that Sally had worn.

Both looked at Patsy's hatted reflection in the cheval glass. "Huh. It doesn't look right on me. What's wrong with me, Sally? Nothing ever looks beautiful on me."

"Likely you choosing the wrong things, Patsy." Sally lifted the offending chapeau from her friend's head. "You sure you want me to tell you what I think?" Sally placed the hat on the side of the high bed.

"Please Sally. I'd do almost anything to look fashionable and pretty."

"Well," Sally took a deep breath, "You so tall and what my mama'd call a 'handsome' woman, like you daddy. You got his red hair, too. I think it right pretty but it...it special, Patsy." She stepped away from the glass and sat in one of the chairs. "He know how to dress to look good, girl."

"It sounds like you're telling me I'd make a good looking man,

Sally. I want to be a pretty woman!"

"I ain't saying..."

"You said 'ain't,' Sally."

"I'm not saying," Sally smiled her thanks at Polly, "That you look like a man...just that you might learn something from a man, from your father." She wrapped her linen apron around her arm, "You can't look like all these other little bitty ordinary women, Patsy. You special. Like him."

"Can you help me look special, Sally?"

"I can do my best, girl. Let's look at your clothes and I tell you what I'd do iffen I was you."

"If I were you."

"Yeah. If I were you. You help me with the talk and I help you with the dressing." Sally stood and put her hand on the older girl's red gold curls, "I'm good with hair, too."

"I want you to help me too, Sally." Polly pulled on Sally's apron. "Make me special, too."

Sally put her arm around Polly's shoulders. "You already special, Miss Polly. You're a real pretty little girl and with your coloring you can wear just about anything." She looked into the blue eyes of the eight year old, "What we going to have to do for you is beautify your vocabulary."

Polly leaned onto Sally's lap to peer earnestly into Sally's face. "You mean no more 'stupid cow,' no more 'Go piss up a rope?'"

Sally couldn't control her laughter.

"That's exactly what I mean."

Patsy began jerking dresses from her tall wooden wardrobe until she had covered the pink satin counterpane with piles of busily ruffled, lace trimmed, embroidered dresses, many white, some yellow, several printed with tiny flowers tossed onto pastel backgrounds.

Sally picked up one of the flowered print dimity frocks and peered from beneath her lashes to be sure Patsy wanted this truth from her. Convinced that the older girl was eager to hear what she had to say she held up the offending dress.

"Take this pretty dimity, Patsy. It just ain't...isn't, for you. This would be just fine for Polly but little bitty prints and teenincey flowers aren't right for your tall frame." Her hand made a sweeping gesture over the piled clothing, "You need to give all these rosebuds to your little sister."

"Tell you what I'll do, Sally. I'll give you one or two, also. Would they look good on you?"

Sally felt herself blush with pleasure. More new clothes! Beautiful new clothes! She knew almost anything would look good on her but she kept that thought to herself.

"What do you think, Miss Patsy?" She held the rose sprigged dress to her shoulders.

Patsy groaned and sat down. "Why don't any of them look like that when I hold them under my chin?"

"Wrong color, wrong style, girl. We going to fix you up right. You going to be able to go out in Paris and make these little old Frenchie girls look sick." Sally put her hand under Patsy's chin and lifted it, "You hold your head high. You a Jefferson. An American. A special looking woman."

"Can we do something about me before teatime, Sally? I'd like to surprise Papa."

"Well, one thing is right here. White's good for you. We just take off all that ruffled stuff and that lace and you'll see. I fix your hair, too."

The two young women and the child spent the rest of the day giggling and sewing and trying hair styles. They talked about Monticello, about Abigail and John Adams and about their ocean trips, with Polly acting out most of the parts, especially the roles of the captain and the sailors. Right up until teatime, a loud and laughing hail of "Bloody shirkers" and "Blasted lags" and "Damned Bastards," filled the feminine air of the rose and white room.

ALL THREE WERE in the parlor before Thomas Jefferson came for his afternoon tea. Patsy sat with her red hair swept back and clubbed off at the nape with an embroidered indigo ribbon. Tiny ringlets fell long at the front of each ear, the rest of her red glory remained elegant simplicity. Her white dress, minus the embroidered lace, was pristine over her indigo petticoats. Polly looked the perfect tiny lady in a yellow flower print over a lace trimmed skirt. The lace kerchief in her little girl bosom and a shortbread dainty in her hand were her bribes for "forgetting" all "sailor talk" while at the teatable.

Sally made ready to pour, wearing the cutdown rose sprigged dimity, her cheeks flaming a deeper rose with the excitement, her shining dark curls piled in seeming abandon atop her head. An embroidered pink moire ribbon threaded its way through the carefree arrangment. When the tall master of the house stepped into the parlor he let his gray gaze travel over each of the three excited girls. He smiled his approval and finally let his attention focus on the one who had the place of honor, the one who began to pour his tea with the natural grace with which she did all things.

He sat in his blue velvet wing chair, stretched his long legs with a sigh that could only be pure relaxation and asked, "What have my three young ladies been up to this day?"

Chapter 15

July 1787

SALLY LIFTED THE teacup and with her gaze directed toward the pale blue Chinese rug, she handed the hot cup of tea to her waiting Master. The lemon brew drifted a spicy scent upon the air. She could feel the steam from the teapot rising against her cheek and she knew her pale skin blushed rosy with the heat. She could almost feel the strands of her hair twirling themselves into a riot of corkscrews as they always did when the air was filled with moisture.

She smiled.

She said nothing.

With her other hand she pressed to touch the small satin bag which hung hidden between her breasts.

"Thank you, Sally Hemings."

"You're welcome, Master Jefferson."

Polly danced across the space between Sally and Thomas Jefferson.

"Father. See my new dress. Sally fixed it for me." She curtsied low to show off the garment then rose and moved to stand at Sally's knee. "And she fixed one for herself and one for Patsy." Attacked by a sudden and unexpected shyness, Polly scurried to hide behind Sally's chair.

"I see," the male voice held the three young women enthralled, "This Sally is a wonder, indeed. Beautiful, soft spoken, and useful as well." Sally raised her gaze in time to see him look full at her, "Your dresses are to be complimented. They are very lucky to be worn by three such charming graces."

"Papa," Sally could hear the struggle in Patsy's words. Sally realized that his words could always make this daughter's world bright or dim. "Do you think my hair looks nice this way? Sally arranged it."

"Stand up and turn around, Miss Martha, let us see the new style."

Patsy stood and turned, her freckles standing out against her whitefaced anxiety.

Jefferson nodded. Smiled. "I like it very well, my dear. I believe you are growing up to be a most charming young woman." He put out a hand. "Come here Polly. Before you become too grownup like your sister, perhaps you would sit on my knee?"

Polly looked at Sally. Sally nodded. The child nodded back then took tiny steps toward the seated man.

"She looks to you for permission, then, Sally Hemings?" He lifted his youngest daughter onto his lap.

Sally kept her gaze lowered. "She's just getting used to you, sire." She smiled a secret smile, "You are, after all, very big and she is, after all, quite small."

Jefferson raised his hand toward the still standing Patsy. "Does my Patsy also have your permission to embrace her father?" Patsy beamed radiantly and moved to stand within the crook of his arm. He smiled from between the happy faces of his children, his gray eyes gleaming with mischief. "And who will give you permission to join our happy band, Sally?"

"It is enough for me, Master Jefferson, to see the three of you together." She cocked her head to one side, "I give my own self leave to enjoy your family's happiness."

He nodded as if he had expected her answer. "The letter I have just received from the Eppes says you are highly intelligent for a sl...servant. I believe Mistress Eppes may be right."

Sally smiled her thanks, her cup poised to drink. A long moment passed as they stared across the tea table at each other. He broke the quiet with a flurry of hugs and questions and answers.

"I have a surprise for you."

"For me?" Polly jumped to the floor and turned to lean against his knee. "A surprise?"

"Yes, for you and your sister."

"For me?" Patsy's face reddened with pleasure.

"Yes, for you. For all of you."

"Sally too?"

"For Sally, also."

"What is it?" Polly shouted and lifted her skirts to do an impromptu hornpipe, "What's our surprise, Father? Is it good to eat?"

"Not food for the stomach but food for the mind."

Patsy's smile faded. "Sounds like school to me." She jerked away from his encircling arm, "I told you, Father, I don't want to go back to

Switzerland."

"School? Ugh." Polly collapsed on the rug. "Fuck the bloody school." Tears welled in her eyes, "And I ain't going nowhere. So there."

"Polly!" Sally pulled the eight year old to stand next to her, "You promised."

"Well, nobody said anything about having to go to a bastardly school." She yanked the lace handerchief from the front of her dress. "Here, you can have it back. I ain't going to no school, Sally, and I'm going to say 'bloody' any damned time I like."

"I'm sorry Master Jefferson. She been too many places already."

Patsy stood frozen at the arm of her father's chair. Polly bent her head to Sally's chest and cried in earnest. Sally looked apologetically at their father.

"Let's not carry on so, girls." Thomas Jefferson stood, a frown etched between his brows. "I've enrolled you in a convent day school right here in Paris." He tried to pull Patsy into his arms again, "You'll be home every night and all day Sunday." He turned a worried face toward Sally as if to enlist her in his cause, "I thought you'd all three be pleased."

"All three of us?" Polly stopped in midsob. "Right here?"

"Of course. I don't want to lose my girls just when I've found them again." He sat in his chair and beckoned his youngest to himself once more. He stroked Polly's back and kept his arm about Patsy but his words were for Sally. "I want you to learn French."

Sally felt a jolt of pleasure. She could learn to speak the language. She could get an education. Maybe she wouldn't be a slave anymore. She could stay here in the house with this tall, broad shouldered man who came to tea in his carpet slippers. She smiled tenderly at his frown.

"Everything going to be all right, Master Jefferson. We'll all go to that school, won't we Patsy?" She looked up at the tall redheaded girl who nodded, unsmiling. She put her hand under the chin of the leaning younger sister. "Polly?"

Polly nodded glumly. "I guess so, if you and Patsy go, Sally."

"I wonder if you girls would loan Sally to me for a moment?" Jefferson smiled at his daughters, "I need to talk to her privately. In my library. You two will please wait for us. In a moment we'll return and finish our tea." He was already striding from the room.

Sally followed. Her stomach felt strange. As if she were swinging high on one of the vines in the woods back in Virginia, going up high and James pushing her still higher. Excited but scared, too.

When her owner sat behind his desk he nodded to the chair in front of it.

"Sit down, Sally Hemings. I have something to tell you." He picked up a sheet of paper from his desk. "Something sorrowful, I'm afraid." His gray eyes shimmered sympathy, "I have heard from our little mountain that your baby sister, Lucy, has died. I'm sorry." He stood abruptly as if the desk were some sort of prison. "I too lost a small Lucy, you remember, so I know something of what you must feel."

Sally tried to think what she felt. Tried to remember Lucy. She couldn't remember anything except a tiny bundle her mother had shown her and said it was her baby sister, Lucy. She tried again, then put Polly's face on the baby. That was sad. That made the tears come all right. Her baby sister Lucy/Polly was dead! She wiped the tears on Polly's lace kerchief then waited to hear what else he had to say. It was pretty clear that he had something else to say, something that made him even sadder than the death of her little sister.

He slumped again into the chair at his desk. "I don't know what to say nor how to say it." He knuckled his dry eyes as if he could rub away what he saw in the letter. "I want to assure you that I've asked that Betty Hemings and your younger brothers, Martin and Bob not be sent." He shot a look of appeal toward her.

Not be sent? Sent where? Sally shivered and moved to the edge of her chair so she wouldn't miss anything.

He was silent another moment.

"I'm having financial difficulties, my dear." Again he rose to pace behind the polished wooden table. "I know that I am sinning greatly by using the devil's invention of slavery as a way out of my dilemma." Again he gave her the look of appeal.

"I don't understand sir. What is it?"

"I have had to send a letter in answer to the one you brought me. To bring in necessary monies all of our slaves have had to be rented out." He grasped his hands behind his back. "You understand I was desperate, Sally Hemings." He circled to stand just in front of the chair where she sat. "God forgive me."

Sally felt frozen in place. Rented out. She remembered the stories she had heard from the older slaves about being "rented out" from other plantations. All the people on Monticello had assured the ones who had suffered while at the same time assuring themselves, "Master Thomas

Jefferson ain't never going to let nothing like that happen to you again. Not here. Not from this here plantation. Here on this mountain we got us a good master."

Jefferson placed a tentative hand on her shoulder. "Your mother will never be rented out, my dear."

Sally felt heated and yet cold at the same time. The hand weighted her in place. She felt a scream rising in her. She wanted to tear the questions from her throat, "And what about me? Will I be sent down the river, too?" She sat as if made of stone.

The hard hand passed to her chin to softly lift her face so that she could not escape his gaze.

"I'm sorry, Sally Hemings. I wish it could be otherwise."

Why can't it be otherwise? Again she wanted to scream. Why do my people have to be whipped, or worked to their knees or die? What about Critta? Was she sent off with the rest? She kept her face still and said nothing but he read her eyes.

"I promise, Sally. This will never, never happen to you nor to your mother."

He moved back to sit at the desk and he shoved the letter into a pile of other paper at the end of the table. He leaned forward and cleared his throat.

"Now, let us talk of happier things."

I hate him. Critta. My sister. She been rented out with all the rest. He does what he wants with all of us. We're in his power. For a minute he cares, then he pushes the anger and sadness and shame to one side just like he pushes a piece of paper. She felt as if stripes of heat and cold were chasing each other up and down her back. The lace kerchief lay clenched in a hard ball in her hand.

She raised her eyes to sear him with her anger and she felt pleased to see him jerk back against his chair as if she'd struck him. The line returned between his brows. His eyelids lowered. The gold of his eyelashes glimmered against the purplish circles under his eyes. Her heart skipped.

Anger at her own weakness filled her. She was feeling pity for him. Pity! She was sorry for a man who could sell her or rent her or kill her if he wished.

She tried to shore up her defenses against the silver gaze which a spoke a silent plea for understanding.

He stood and once again came around to where she sat. He put out his hands. She dropped the sodden kerchief in her lap and lifted her hands to rest one in each of the large freckled offerings. Well, maybe he was sorry.

"Tell me, beautiful Sally. Just how do you view me?"

"As my master." But she smiled to take the sting from her words.

"I don't know whether to be sad or happy with your words, my dear." He gave her hands a gentle squeeze and allowed her to remove herself from his grasp.

"You know the French don't understand our domestic...uh... institutions." He toyed with the crystal paperweight that lay near the edge of the desk. "It would, perhaps, be better if we did not press our way of life upon them."

"What are you asking me, Master?"

"Can you let yourself become a part of our family here? Not as a slave?" He lowered his gaze from her searching look. "I want you to act as something between a servant and a...a daughter." He cleared his throat once more. "You will go where my daughters go, do what they do...as a...perhaps as a...a 'friend` of the family, let us say." He smiled broadly, "As a sort of a doyenne, you will keep an eye on the two of them for me. Does that arrangement suit you, my pretty Sally?"

His eyes held hers until she nodded her agreement.

"Shall we return to our tea?"

She stood and the sodden wad of lace dropped to the floor to lie unremarked under the corner of the rosewood desk. They walked toward the parlor. Again he led the way and again, she followed.

Chapter 16

August 1787

SALLY LOOKED across the mound of the gray velvet dress she was remaking for Patsy. She had ripped out lace and torn off ruffles and removed bows. She thought of it as "defussing" the garment. The owner of the dress sat at the pianoforte and played a lively tune so Polly could dance. Thomas Jefferson lounged in an easy chair, a few feet from them, reading. Always reading.

She couldn't understand the need to be always reading or writing. Reading books, yes. Sometimes that was fun, even exciting, but the master read long letters, tedious deeds, or even duller, state papers. When he wasn't reading he was often entertaining visitors. Solemn men wearing dark coats and drab breeches. A few affected the ugly, new long trousers.

Thank heavens the master wore decent blue or fawn colored knee breeches and matching silk hose. With his embroidered satin vests and beautiful blue or gray or fawn colored tailcoats, he put them all to shame, those visitors. His bright hair. As if he carried a light inside his head. Tall. Broad shouldered.

All in all, she decided, the very best looking man in any gathering. The Europeans looked little, squatty, overdressed, compared to the master; the Americans mostly roughly dressed or careless in appearance. Yes. The master outshone them all in every possible way.

She stared at the long legs thrust forward from under the writing table. His legs were a series of delicious long curves, sheathed in pale silk. He was proud of his legs...and rightly so. The breeches showed his strong calves to their very best advantage.

She bit a last thread and held the gray dress up for a last inspection.

If only he wouldn't wear carpet slippers. His black slippers with the silver buckles looked so elegant.

Her eyes sent an angry message to the worn house shoes. "You the only things that keep him from looking quite perfect. Why don't you go and lose yourselves, old slippers?"

She lifted her gaze to see the man staring at her over the sheaf of papers in his hand. His look held her in place, not moving, for a second, two seconds, long moments. He gestured silently toward his library.

She let the now simpler gown pouf itself to one side and she followed him down the hall. In the library they sat in their usual places, he at his writing table, she in the wooden armchair facing him.

"How are my daughters doing in school, Sally?"

"Very well, sir, I think. Polly may even learn some naughty French words to replace her sailor language." She smiled.

"And you Sally. How about you? Do you like the school?"

"Like it?" She questioned herself inwardly, Do I like it? "I am so glad to go to school, Master Jefferson, I would go whether I liked it or not."

He rose and stepped to a cabinet in the corner of the room.

"I've brought you something, pretty Sally." He held up a bolt of fine, deep crimson silk. "I want you to have it. Perhaps you or the French seamstress could make a dress or two from this." He let a river of silk flow into Sally's lap. "The color is not suitable for Patsy and the silk is much too luxurious for an eight year old," His gray eyes twinkled, "That leaves only one of my girls that could use such stuff."

Sally's heart thumped joy. His girls.

"Oh, sir. It's so beautiful."

"Like you. The truth, my dear, is that I bought it only two days ago...and I bought it just for you."

"How can I thank you?"

He was silent for a moment, put his finger to his lips as if cogitating on her question.

"How best can a young lady thank a gentleman who is twice...uh, almost twice her age?" His arms closed about the air in front of him. "An embrace, perhaps? A light kiss, perhaps? I'll let the young lady decide."

Sally let her silken burden slide to the floor. She kept her gaze downcast, but she smiled a secret smile as she entered the open arms.

"I think an embrace and a light kiss, sir."

She raised her face to the brush of his lips against her own, his hands warm upon her back. His lips felt dry, but alive; cool, yet clinging for a moment. The scent of him filled her. She took a breath of him then put her cheek against his embroidered waistcoat and spoke softly against his chest. "Yes. I think another kiss, master. Another one, sir." She raised her head again and put one hand to his neck and guided him again to her lips. This time his lips relaxed, opened slightly, moistened a bit against her own. Her hardening nipples pressed against the cloth of her dress as if they too sought the sculptured lips of the man.

"I love the red silk, sir."

"Can you call me Tom when we are alone, my little Sally?"

She stepped back from the encircling arms, daring in her voice.

"Yes, Tom. I can...if you can call me, 'Mistress Sally' when we are alone."

Laughing she swept up the silk and hurried to Polly's room. After carefully placing the bolt of cloth in the trunk that sat at the foot of her cot, she ran to the mirror which rested on the dresser in the bowed window.

Huge dark eyes stared a question back at her. What had just happened in there? No more pretense of mere fatherly interest. The game was quickening. Her stomach lurched.

"Be careful," she warned herself. She could remember her mother's words, "You got youth and beauty and your maidenhood, girl. Mayhaps, if'n you're smart too, those things be enough."

THE LANGUOR OF Paris in August was somehow different than the heated torpor she remembered from Monticello in the summer. Sally walked along the pathway in the convent garden, arm in arm with Patsy.Sally enjoyed seeing her own new green dimity and ecru lace ruffled sleeve and Patsy's blue and white striped butterfly sleeve make a flurry of color and movement between them. The sedate sounding pattern of their steps broke against the rock retaining wall when Polly suddenly jumped from a low hanging branch to the wall and then to the walk in front of them.

"Polly! You know you aren't supposed to be over here. This walk is for the 'big girls.' You'll get all of us in trouble with Madame." Patsy's voice was a horrified murmur. Sally and Patsy moved quickly to use their wide skirts to form a protective barrier around the smaller child. "You'd better get on back to your own side of the yard." Patsy peered over her shoulder as if the headmistress might be standing on the walk behind them.

Polly leaned back against the wall, a hunted look on her face. "Everybody in this dodrotted place speaks French."

"Polly!" Patsy's voice was a muted scream. "You simply must quit talking that way."

"Why?" Polly twirled the lace ends on the fichu collar of her yellow dimity dress. "What difference does it make? No one around here can understand me anyway."

"She's right, you know," Sally defended the younger sister, "We could be speaking Greek for all the folks around here know...or care." She pulled the lace from Polly's hand and pressed it against the child's chest, "You'll tear that lace, child."

"I don't care. I could just as soon be in a linsey woolsey shift. It'd be a lot less trouble and I don't think the sisters or the other girls ever even look at me." She flipped the lace up to let it droop across her shoulder. "No one to talk to, no one to play with."

Patsy nodded agreement. "It's us against them, you know. Ten minutes a day walking in the garden and the rest of the day sitting in silence while those old dogs bark in French." She smoothed her sister's lace fichu back into place and sighed. "If I didn't have you and Sally, Polly, I don't know what I'd do."

"Maybe we can get your father to let us quit." Sally glanced over her shoulder to be sure the nun with the long, limber switch wasn't in their vicinity. The skinny sister used the switch whenever she heard any words that weren't French. Sally felt especially sorry for the one girl from somewhere in Africa. That poor black girl really didn't have anyone to talk to...not in her own language. If she didn't learn to speak French she'd have to endure a life of silence because she was the only one of her tribe living here in the convent. "Maybe he'd let us study at home."

"He won't." Patsy's voice was querulous. "He wants us busy here everyday so he can do as he pleases." Patsy's face turned somber. "That old Maria Cosway."

Sally felt her heart turn over in her chest, "What about Maria Cosway?"

Patsy and Polly seemed to consult each other without speaking. "You tell her, Patsy." The younger sister nudged her elder, "You're the one that read the damned letter."

"A letter from Mistress Cosway?"

"She ain't our mistress, Sally, and don't you forget it." Polly picked up a stick from beside the path and whaled her words into the stone wall. "She thinks she's the Queen of Sheba but she ain't nobody."

"Isn't," Sally corrected without thinking.

"Isn't, Ain't, what do I care? None of these bitches can understand me and Maria Cosway ain't never going to get even one chance to listen to me." Polly whacked the wall again. "I'll make her life hell if she even dares to come to our house."

Patsy's voice was very low, almost a whisper. "She's coming to Paris this month. She'll be staying in Princess Lubomirski's villa but it's papa she's coming to see." Patsy glanced over her shoulder again. "That's what she said in the letter."

Sally swallowed the frustrated anger that rose to her lips. So. Master Jefferson had been so sweet these past weeks for nothing. Oh. Silks and kisses. He had been nice for a reason...just not the reason that she had thought. He wanted someone to look after his daughters whilst he dallied with this European lady, Maria Cosway. Sally wished desperately that she too had a stick with which to beat the wall.

"She's coming to see Master Thomas Jefferson?"

"What's the matter with you, Sally? That's what the letter said. I told you. That's why we're at this pissant school, I expect."

Sally took the stick from Polly and tossed it over the stone wall.

"You'd better get on back, Polly. Exercise time about over, I expect." She and Patsy kept Polly hidden behind their skirts as they glided toward the area where the younger children played. "Patsy and I will talk this over. We'll see you after classes this afternoon. Now, scat."

They stood and watched the younger girl slink toward the back entryway which the smaller children were required to use. A white coiffed sister barred the way and forced the American child back to the walk below, berating her in French at each step.

"She's telling her it's still two minutes until they are to come inside," Patsy muttered, "Sometimes I have to agree with Polly. This place is full of bitches who speak French."

"I want to learn French." Sally spoke more fiercely than she had intended, "I will learn French, but this isn't the only place in the world to do that."

Patsy leaned closer to Sally. "Are you going to quit the school? What are you going to tell my Father?" Excitement crept into her voice, "Are you going to talk to him tonight?"

"No. Not tonight. Tonight I have something else I need to do." She touched the lace trimmed dimity fichu at her chest to feel the satin juujuu bag against her breast. "But soon, Patsy. Soon, I will tell your father several things. About you two. About school. About his woman friend. About me. About himself."

Whirling through the darkness of his library, carrying one small candle, inner self sparkling with angry life, "Maria Cosway, Maria Cosway," Sally Hemings murmured, and she made the name an ominous song as she twirled.

Chapter 17

October 1787

"DID YOU TALK to our father?" Polly kicked her bed covers off to the floor, "Have you asked him about us quitting the school?"

"Not yet, Polly." Sally finished spreading the coverlets on her own cot then began making up Polly's high bed. "He's been gone so much I've hardly seen him."

"Yeah. Damn old Maria Cosway's eyes. Woman's sailing too close to the wind." Polly tossed a handful of water into her face then dried on the linen towel. "You need to do something, Sally. Take the wind out of the bitch's sails."

"Well, I'll do my best, child, if you'll quit acting and talking like some old tar just off the ship." She winked at the smaller girl.

Polly laughed. "I'm glad you're staying in my room, Sally."

"So am I. It's always good to have company. Let's get ourselves down to breakfast, child. Maybe your father will eat with us since it's Sunday." She moved to the clothes press and brought out a two piece blue and white flowered dimity with white lace panniers for the youngest Jefferson. "I'll wear my new dimity dress, too."

"These dresses aren't new. Just Patsy's made over."

"New to us. We ought to be happy to have them. They're so pretty."

"Why does my father buy Patsy so many clothes? Her wardrobe and the clothes press in her room are just stuffed with dresses and hats."

"Likely he want her to look pretty, child. And after all, she is the oldest...his first born. First born always got privileges." Sally tied a bow at Polly's waistline. "She getting almost old enough to be his official hostess, you know."

"What's that?" Polly turned and preened in the looking glass she held in one hand. "Am I going to be one?"

"Probably. Someday. When you marry some nice man and he wants you to meet his guests." Sally slipped pale dimity ruffles over her head, muffling her voice, "A hostess sees that a man's friends have what they need or want while they visit or talk business...you know, like the men when they come to see Master Jefferson?" She grunted with the effort of pulling the thin garment down. "You better help me."

Polly put the mirror onto the table and yanked on the lacey hem of the dress to pull the starched frock down over Sally's breasts.

Sally turned her back to the child, "Now my sash, Polly. Can you tie it without wrinkling it?" Polly nodded and with her tongue held between her teeth she worked to make a perfect "butterfly" bow.

"I did it just the way you showed me."

"Thanks. Get our shawls and we'll go. You ready?"

"Yeah. But I don't understand about Patsy being his hostess. You're the one always talking and smiling and handing 'round the tea, 'specially since he hurt his hand while he was riding. He always calls on you." She shivered her distaste. "Bunch of boring old farts, anyway."

She placed her hand in Sally's outstretched one, "Patsy hates them as much as I do."

"Well, I guess you and Patsy are glad I'm there to talk to your father's guests?" A momentary confusion fluttered in Sally's consciousness. It's true. I am always the one Master Jefferson calls on when he has men to the house. When he has couples or women he calls for Patsy, with me to help her. She shoved the thought from her mind so she wouldn't have to examine it too closely.

"Good morning ladies," the sober masculine voice belied the twinkling gray eyes of the man at the head of the table. "Late for breakfast, I see."

Polly ran to his side and reached to put a light kiss on Thomas Jefferson's cheek. "Come on, Sally. Why don't you give him a kiss on the cheek, too? He'd like that, wouldn't you father?"

Sally felt the heat rising in her face. She kept her eyes downcast. "Polly, for heaven's sake."

Jefferson spoke again, his voice still grave but a smile twitched at the corner of his lips. "I think I would like that, Polly. Thank you for thinking of such a nice thing for me." He lifted his uninjured hand and beckoned Sally with a gesture to his cheek. "Right here, if you please, Mistress Sally."

"See Sally. He's calling you Mistress Sally. He's making you his hostess." The child shoved Sally forcefully toward the seated man.

Sally bent and touched her lips to the smoothly cool, freckled cheek. She straightened and looked her Master in the face. He turned his countenance so she could reach the other cheek and he gestured for a second kiss. His gaze compelled her to touch her lips to his skin once again, this time for a moment longer.

"Thank you, my dear."

Sally looked up to see Patsy standing transfixed in the doorway.

Jefferson smiled and called to her,"Come in, let us eat, daughter."

Patsy filled her plate and sat down at her father's right hand without a word, her eyes huge in her white face. Sally silently filled her own plate and took her usual place next to Polly. The younger sister chattered and laughed throughout the meal but her father and the two older girls spoke only the polite necessities.

When Jefferson stood to quit the table he made an announcement. "I've arranged for all of you to be inoculated for smallpox. The doctor will be here for tea. You should all wear things which allow you to bare your left arms." He turned and left the room without another word.

"What's 'inoculate' mean, Sally?"

Sally leveled her gaze across the table at Patsy. "Do you want to talk about it, girl?"

"Why were you kissing papa?"

"Both Polly and your father wanted me to...and I wanted to do so." Her hand touched the juujuu bag. Careful, she warned herself, Patsy always was mighty jealous of her pa.

"What's wrong with you, Patsy?" Polly scrambled up to kneel in her chair, her elbows resting on the table, "Don't you want Sally to like father?"

"Like him? Yes. Kiss him? I don't know." The older girl smoothed a red curl back into her white morning cap as Sally had taught her. "I felt funny."

Sally also leaned to place her elbows on the table. Might as well get everything out in the open right now, she thought. He's not going to be any help.

"Well, you two girls want me to get rid of Mistress Cosway. You want me to keep your father happy. You want me to persuade the man to stay here at home with us." She knitted her fingers together in front of her as if she were praying. "I'll need both of you to help me do these things. We can't work this out if we aren't all in agreement."

Patsy shrank back in her chair. "You mean..." She glanced quickly at Polly. "You mean...you're going to take Maria Cosway's place?" She looked a little like a startled young animal.

Sally felt a twinge of pity for her old friend. "One thing being a slave does for you, Patsy. It teach you to see what's real."

"What's real? And what does 'inoculate' mean?" Polly tugged at Sally's sleeve.

Sally laid an arm across Polly's shoulder. "What's real is that your father is a strong man. Still young acting. He need a woman." She looked across at Patsy. "And I guess Patsy going to have to tell you what 'inoculate' mean."

"It's Lister's new medicine to keep us from getting smallpox." Patsy said, then sat in silence for a moment, seemingly adding up the figures Sally had laid before her. "Well, I really hate Madame Cosway."

"Me too, Patsy." Polly took the opportunity to dump huge spoonsful of sugar into her tea. She stirred the sweet concoction with happy concentration. "The bloody bitch."

"I feel the same way...but your father thinks he loves her, I reckon."

"Ugh."

"You Jefferson girls want her being mama to you?"

"No." It was a chorus of two.

"Where you think he goes when he spends two, three days away from home?" Sally pushed the question, knowing she was hurting Patsy but not knowing what else to do. "You think he meeting with a bunch of old men to talk about tariff?"

Patsy whispered the only answer she could. "No."

"Well then, what you want me to do?"

Polly poured tea into her saucer. "I vote to make old Maria Cosway walk the plank." She made the same sort of satisfying slurping sound that her father did each morning. "I like tea better with sugar. Plenty of sugar."

"Well, Sally, you do belong to our family. You are our mother's sister, after all." Patsy began her evaluation of the situation. "You're our friend, too...aren't you?"

"Sally's our mother's sister?" Polly set her saucer down so hard it sloshed brown drops onto the white linen cloth. "Isn't she a slave?"

"Yes, to both questions." Patsy's smile toward her young sister was a study in distraction. "Our Grandfather, John Wayles was mother's father but he was Sally Hemings' father also. Now be quiet a minute, Polly. Just let us think."

"That makes her our aunt? Sally's our aunt? Like Aunt Eppes? Yay." Polly stood up to dance a jig in her chair. "Hurrah! I'm going to call her, Aunt Sally."

"You'll do nothing of the kind." Patsy's reprimand sounded almost absent minded.

Sally sat unspeaking, holding the small satin bag tightly against her breast. Her gaze never veered from Patsy's face. She look so much like him, she thought, 'specially when she's troubled.

"Will if I want to. You're my Aunt Sally, aren't you?" The eight year old shoved her plate aside and sat on the table so she could peer into Sally's face. "That's why we look alike, ain't it?"

"Isn't it." Sally nodded agreement even as she corrected.

"See, Patsy?"

"Will you make me...us, some promises, Sally?" Patsy moved around to her father's chair. She motioned impatiently to the maid who stuck her head into the room. "*Vienez plus tard.*" She bent her head toward Sally's. "Are you willing to make a vow?"

"I will if I can, Patsy. You and me, we made a vow a long time ago, girl. Likely you forgot. Remember our blood on our thumbs," Sally held up her left thumb,"And our promise to each other, 'Friends forever'?"

"You two made a blood vow?" Polly's question held awe. "Can I make one, too?"

"You wouldn't want to have your thumb cut."

"Would too."

"What kind of vow did you have in mind, Patsy?"

"Oh, something like, 'friends forever' or 'us against the Cosway' or 'we'll always put family first.' How does that sound?"

"Sounds fine to me," Sally felt herself smiling inwardly. Everything was going to be all right. Patsy was still her old easily led friend and Polly would be on her side no matter what. "Shall I go get a sharp knife from the kitchen?"

Patsy gave a solemn nod and Polly shouted "Yes," from her seat on the table.

When Sally returned with a small, razor sharp paring knife, the three heads huddled over the slicing of each thumb, black hair, brown hair and red hair intermingled as closely as the blood they exchanged on their three left thumbs. "Family forever," each muttered as they touched blood to blood.

"Now Sally," Patsy wrapped her thumb in a linen napkin, "I'm going to tell you some good news. Maria Cosway's husband is in London right now. He's in a fit of jealous rage because old Maria has been here in London seeing father."

"How do you know?"

"Well, you know he has me help in the library sometimes. I just read the letters and notes she sends to him. She said it was going to be hard for them to get together now."

Pure pleasure streamed through Sally's thoughts. It's working. Mama's stuff is working. It won't be long now. I got to be ready.

ON MONDAY morning all three girls stayed at home in their beds, each bearing a huge suppurating blister- like sore on her left arm, each feverish and chilled by turns.

"No school for you ladies, today." Sally's brother, James Hemings, delivered to each of the bedrooms the spoken message from Thomas Jefferson. "You're to stay in bed until you're feeling better." He grinned at his sister on her cot. "You too, Sally Hemings. You're to stay home and get waited on just like one of the Jefferson girls. By the Frenchies. Mast' Jefferson say. He say he look in on youall later."

A BIT OF something pinched between thumb and forefinger and withdrawn from the miniature satin bag became defiant dust in the glimmering flare of her rage. With a sweeping gesture in the air from high above her head to the night colors at her heels, she allowed the crumbling juujuu mixture to mark the moment.

Her left hand pressed the still full black satin pouch strongly against the ivory skin between her breasts, even as her right hand scattered the grains of vengence.

"Mast' Jefferson. Thomas Jefferson. Tom. Hear me." The words keened in the place where they'd met so often. She dipped to the floor at the spot where he'd kissed her, then twisted her way upward again, a hiss purling from between her lips.

"Fini. Fini." She jerked a piece of paper from her pocket. Two names. She ripped the names apart and stamped and danced upon the piece inscribed "Maria Cosway" then held it to the flame of the single candle. Ashes to her hand, then broadcast once again to the floor beneath her feet.

She assigned the piece showing "Thomas Jefferson," the invisible place in the air which still held the echo of their kiss. She then folded the name into tiny squares and swooped it into the satin charm bag.

Panting, silent, she closed her eyes and let the velvet darkness sooth her anger and kept her secret.

Chapter 18

"ARE YOU STILL in pain, my dear?" Thomas Jefferson looked at the scabbed over circle on Sally's forearm. She held up the lace ruffle of her sleeve so he could inspect the healing innoculation.

"Not so much, sir. Now it itch me some when the lace touch it."

"Don't scratch, child. You don't want to have any larger scar than you can help." He smoothed the skin around the ugly lesion with his good hand. His touch felt cool and soothing against the heat that emanated from the area of the 'cow pox' inoculation.

"Like ivory satin, little Sally, your skin." He stopped the movement of his hand to take her hand in his. "Let us strive to keep it beautiful." His voice lowered. "Don't worry. Even should you have a large scar it won't really matter, you would be still be beautiful to me, my dear. A scar on one's arm is nothing...nothing." He paused as if he wanted to say something else but he remained silent, his hand tracing the veins that pulsed in her wrist.

"Thank you, sir." Her words were whispered. What was it he wanted to say? What should she answer? Her gaze was caught by the rich gleam of the handrubbed, wooden balustrade. She felt the impulse to pull herself away, to flee up the stairs to Polly's room, to safety, to turn back to childhood before it was too late. But she stood still, forced herself to stand, unmoving.

He brought his own injured hand to the light. "I live every day with the knowledge that my hand will probably never really heal. Something torn inside, no doubt." He turned the curling fingers up for her inspection. "Does the sight of such a claw repel you, child?"

Sally grasped the withering fingers in both of her own and touched the back of his hand with her lips. "No part of you could ever repel me, sir." She massaged the injured digits, "May I try some of the medicines Betsy Hemings taught me? A curing salve? Mayhaps we can do more than your physician has been able to do."

He smiled into her eyes and nodded. He pulled the offending hand from her grasp and lifted it to smooth her rioting curls.

"I can still use the thing a little and I can feel the silk of your hair as I touch it."

"Then life is still in your hand, sir."

"I wish your words to be true, little Sally. I have a friend, a lady, who swears to be my friend...and yet, she says she is repulsed by this claw." His smile held sadness. "Would not wish to be touched by it."

"This lady is no friend, sire, if the results of a small riding accident can cause her to be so delicate in her sensibilities." Sally raked his person with a bold glance. "You are a fine figure of a man, Master Jefferson, a bad hand does not change that."

"Thank you, my dear. And even with an itching scab on your arm you are a beautiful, beautiful youngster."

Sally lowered her gaze. "How nice of you to say so, sire."

"We are alone now, Sally, Mistress Sally. You promised to call me 'Tom,' did you not?"

"I did, Tom." She looked him fully in the eye. "May I venture to guess whether the lady in question might be Maria Cosway?"

Sally felt the sharp sting of satisfaction at the look of shock that passed across his face. He swallowed and paused a moment before he spoke. His voice was dry, almost a whisper.

"I did not know you were even aware of the existence of Madame Cosway."

Madame Cosway! Putting me in my place, Sally told herself. She realized that the rasped sentence also held a touch of anger. He's angry about old Cosway's rejection of him and he's going to try to take it out on me.

"Well, tell me sir, is she the woman who thinks an injured hand so disgusting?" A little pressure might be to the good. Let him think about what is really happening with this European witch.

He nodded without speaking.

"Then may I speak boldly, Tom?" She softened her request with the hint of dimples in one cheek.

He nodded again.

"You'd be well rid of a woman who finds your injured member repulsive, who is disliked by your family, who is a European, and who is, after all, a married woman."

His grunt of surprise pleased Sally. He needs to know I'm a woman, too. A woman who knows what's happening in his world. A woman who is concerned about him. She kept her vision trained on his face. The anger there was chased by other emotions...surprise, curiosity, and interest.

"You know much about me, Mistress Sally. I would learn more

about you."

She sent another flirt of the dimple. "More about me, Tom?"

"Yes, you little darling. You are quite beguiling." He enclosed her in his arms. "Mayhaps I have been searching elsewhere when I should have been looking right here at home." He traced a dark curl that lay across the lace trimming her fichu. Her breast felt the heat of the tracery as if a flame had touched her and she knew her nipples hardened, longing for something more from this man.

Sally let her hand smooth the gray satin of his waistcoat then with the flash of a thumbnail she drew a symbol she'd learned from her mother just over his heart before she raised her face to meet his.

She knew this kiss was different than the others had been. He seemed to turn his full attention on her, all else forgotten. His mouth opened against hers and she answered with a small sigh of surrender. He tasted like the sweet black coffee she had just watched him drink at breakfast.

She felt herself turn into pure feeling, all life concentrated in the touch, the taste and the hardness of him. She could love this man. Deeply, deeply. She knew it in the deepest part of herself. Wings of excitement beat behind her breasts, her breath caught within the heat of his kiss, her body melted against him. Yes, let him compel her. She'd no longer any will of her own.

Thomas Jefferson drew his face away from hers, his indrawn breath a sharply sent sign of his excitement.

"My God, Sally."

Sally let her heavy eyelids drift open, let her body return to where they stood in the front hallway. For a second she stared at his face. As if from a distance she heard her mother's voice. "This your chance. Do the thing right, girl."

He again moved as if to kiss her once more but she stepped back from the circle of his arms.

"What's wrong, my Sally? Come. Let me kiss you again."

"You want more than a kiss."

"I do. And so do you."

"No sir."

"This is what you want too, Sally, darling."

He could force me do this, she thought. He's forgotten. Good. Now is my time. Once he's had his way all my needs will be forgotten. Let him suffer for his pleasure. He will enjoy all the more.

"No sir. I beg you to put such a thing from your mind. I cannot do as you wish."

"Why not?"

"There is something in the way of our..." She paused and looked down, letting her eyelashes sweep against her cheeks before she again raised her gaze to meet his.

His face reddened. "Then what do you want?"

"Oh, Tom. I'm not looking for gifts or special attention. You've always been very kind to me." She let the lashes fall again to the cheeks. "It's just that I cannot, in good conscience, kiss a man who loves another."

"Loves another?" The tall man looked stupified. "What are you talking about?"

"I think you know."

"Maria Cosway?"

She nodded.

"Madame Cosway has already absented herself from London, my dear. I believe she has returned to her husband." The pain that crossed his face tore also at Sally's heart. "She left so swiftly that we had no chance to say farewell." So. He still wished for the Cosway woman. Perhaps with the right kind of luck she could turn that interest in her own direction. She touched the satin bag that rested on her breast.

"But you wish to see her yet again it seems."

"If I send Madame Maria Cosway from me will you kiss me then, Sally?"

"We can at least talk about it then, Thomas."

"I will write her a note this very hour."

"To tell her you can never see her again?"

"Never see her again." The line between his brows deepened. "That's what you want?"

"That's what we all want...Patsy, Polly and I."

His gray eyes caught light with the exciting implication of what she was telling him. "Then everything is arranged?"

"We will talk. Later." She felt the momentary prick of guilt. Polly was on her side. Patsy might not care so much for the reality of their plan. She shrugged. Patsy could be persuaded. "Perhaps there are some other things I will require of you." She favored him with the light touch of her palm against his lips. "Perhaps there are things you will want to do for me."

He caught her hand in his own and brought it again to his lips. "If you wish I'll show you the letter before James takes it to be delivered to the lady's door." He touched her hand to his lips once more. "Would you care to see the missive, my little Sally?"

She nodded, her heart pounding with triumph.

"Then you shall...within the hour."

She turned toward the curved stairway. With the sweeping movement she had seen Mistress Eppes use at Monticello, she gracefully gathered up her brightly checked dimity skirts and her quilted taffeta underskirt with one hand, the hand with the vacinated arm. She did not hurry. She let the fingers of her free hand trail along the gleaming, satiny wood of the delicately carved bannister. Her touch stirred the light, clear scent of beeswax. She held her head high. Even though she didn't look back she felt the man's silver gaze piercing her until she had moved completely onto the second floor landing and out of his sight. She felt quite certain that he remained staring upward long moments after she had disappeared.

She stood silently for a heartbeat. Then she grinned, dropped her ladylike composure and with both hands she wadded her billowing skirts into a careless ball, then galloped, two steps at a time, up the remaining flight of stairs toward Polly's room.

Chapter 19

November 1787

"DRAT," AS HE muttered the word, Jefferson peered at Sally over the edge of a small square, white, envelope. He handed the just delivered letter to her without comment. She, equally silent, glanced at it. She noted that it was written in a feminine hand before she tossed it back to him. She didn't read the note.

"I thought you'd want to read it."

"Apparently you wanted to read it, sir. It is nothing to me. You must do as you wish."

"It's from Madame Cosway."

"I assumed as much."

"She says she has commissioned Trumbull to paint a portrait of me. What do you think of that?"

"I think nothing of it, sir. Madame Maria Cosway is your friend." She placed the sheaf of letters she had been working with onto his desk. "I'll file these for you later, sir, or have Petit do it." She straightened the papers into a neat stack. "I've just remembered I promised Patsy and Polly we'd study together this evening."

"But Sally, what am I...?"

She quietly closed the study door to cut off his next words, then descended to the kitchen. When she came back up and into the parlor where the girls waited she carried a tray. Polly stood and peered into first one, then the other of the dishes on the tray.

"Bloody good, I say, Sally. You've brought us some good stuff to nibble on."

Patsy leaned over the tray also.

"Sister, you're a little girl now but if you keep being so greedy, how many stone will you weigh when you're my age?" Patsy too lifted napkins and chose a sweet. "Put the tray on the table between us, Sally, or you and I won't get a thing."

"You two ready to parse some verbs?" Sally chose the chair

nearest the silver candlelabra. Of the six candles in the holder, only two were lit. "Don't we need some light?"

"Father says we must economize." Patsy's lips were prim over the words.

"I don't care if I can't see what I'm writing." Polly waved two prizes in the air. "I can see this cold mutton sandwich and this pickle and that's enough for me."

"Let's allow Master Jefferson to economize in some other way." Sally touched one of the lit tapers to the waiting four. "Now, we can see to work." She smiled at her two friends. "Shall we practice on Petit or shall we just work with each other?"

"No Frenchies." The mutton and biscuit disappeared in three bites. Half the pickle followed.

"I'd rather work without his help, also, Sally. He seems so...so forward."

The rote exercises Sally laid out for the three of them allowed her to work even as she examined her pain. Not pain, she corrected herself, her anger. He had obviously been seeing the Cosway again. Afraid I'd find the letter, likely, she mused, and I would have. Well, he the one who have to make the choice now. I ain't...I'm not saying another word to him about the woman. And not another kiss, not another touch. I've set up my rules. Now he can win the game or lose it.

The ominously heavy quiet from the study made her quiver with anticipation. What would he do now? Before they had covered one verb she had her answer.

"Mistress Sally," The words thundered from the study.

Sally excused herself to the two younger Jeffersons then stood and ambled toward the other room. At the still closed door she knocked and spoke.

"Yes, Mr. Jefferson. What can I do for you, sir?"

"Get in here!"

Sally smiled over her shoulder at the two watching girls before she opened the study door. Once inside she kept one hand on the doorknob.

"Yes sir. I'm here."

"Close that door."

"Certainly sir." She closed the door and leaned against it. "What was it you needed, sir?"

"Are you trying to drive me crazy?"

"No sir. I'm trying to attend to my school work."

"Sod the schoolwork."

"Oh, Mr. Jefferson, sir. You mustn't speak in such a way. You're setting a bad example for Miss Polly."

Jefferson sighed and looked at the note on the desk before him. In the light from the candles on his desk, Sally could see the fine blue veins in his eyelids. She could also see the blood vessel flutter in his forehead. Angry. Good. So was she. He was only getting what he deserved.

He peered up at her through golden red brows. "Sally. You're trying to make me suffer...and you're succeeding." He lifted his hands as if in defeat. "I am miserable if that's what you want."

"Not at all, sir."

"What happened to 'Tom'?" He gestured her closer.

"He is busy with his lady friend, I expect, sir." She remained in place, her back touching the door.

He had to laugh, then his voice rose to a pleading note.

"I thought we were good friends, Sally girl."

"Oh, no sir."

"No?" Pleading was replaced by astonishment, "We aren't friends?"

"Oh, no sir."

"I thought...you said we...well, if you aren't my friend, what are you?"

Sally lowered her lashes.

"I work for you, sir. I watch over your daughters."

Jefferson pushed the papers on his desk forward as he shoved his chair violently back. His desk candles guttered and died. The acrid odor of hot wax and smoking wick floated in the air. The candles in the wall sconces flickered, then recovered. Thomas Jefferson became a dark and faceless figure against their pale light. Fear traced a feathery line down Sally's arms.

Had she gone too far?

"Sally!" His voice roared through the room.

"Go back to your correspondence, sir. I must do my lessons, sir." She let her voice drop. Gently now, she told herself. Let him do all the shouting and growling.

"Are the damnable lessons more important than I am?"

"Oh, no sir. I must do the lessons because I know you want me to do well." She tipped her head to a submissive pose. "Don't you?"

He threw his hands into the air in a gesture of surrender.

"All right. All right. I'll try to do what you want." He turned his back to her. "I've already told Madame Cosway that I would allow the portrait." He peered over his shoulder at her, "But after that is finished I'll tell her I can never see her again. Will that satisfy you?"

"Whatever you do satisfies me, sir." Lashes down. "Why should I try to tell my master what to do?"

"Oh, Sally, Sally," He shook his head slowly back and forth and chuckled almost silently. "You are a little she-devil." He turned back to face her. "If you'll let me touch you just once more I'll try to be satisfied...for now."

Sally glided toward the desk, touched his cheek, felt heated roughness of unshaven skin, then raced back to the door where she turned. "I await the day when Madame Cosway is no longer between us."

He lifted one hand in a defeated gesture of dismissal. I should feel triumphant, she thought, but I feel...cheated...as though I cheated myself with my little games.

Back at the table with the two girls, Sally tried to turn her mind away from the scene in Tom's office. As the lesson progressed, Polly drooped and laid her head on the table. Patsy droned the French verb exercise. Sally repeated each word.

The door of Jefferson's study flung itself back against the wall and Thomas Jefferson stalked toward their table.

"I don't want you to go to that school anymore. From now on, Mistress Sally, you can study French right here. I need you here." He stalked back to his study.

"May we quit the school, also, papa?" Patsy's voice trembled.

Jefferson pointed toward the stairs. "Up with you and not another word."

The three girls gathered up their books and papers and with hardly a sound they scattered. Polly, sleepily, and Patsy, tearfully, wended their way up to their bedrooms, Sally trotted down to the kitchen.

She put the tray on the worktable in the kitchen and she fingered the juujuu bag at her breast as she stared sightlessly at the huge fireplace used for all the household cookery. For a second she was back at Monticello in the dirt floored cabin she'd shared with her mother.

"You made yourself a juujuu, girl?"

Sally had felt a bit embarrased to show the tiny chips of felt she had put into the silken sack. Betsy Hemings had smiled and asked to keep the charm for a day or two.

"Gonna help you iffen I can, girl. See canst I work up a little something more for you."

Words from the man Petit interuppted her reverie and pulled her back to the Paris kitchen. He spoke simple French and he spoke slowly, as if he wanted to be sure she understood.

"You know, Mademoiselle Sally, even though you may be a slave in that faraway Virginia of yours, here, in my beautiful France, here you are free and you will always be free. A free woman. It is our law. Do not forget that."

Her breath caught in her throat. Free? In France she wasn't a slave? Could that really be true?

Chapter 20

March 1788

"WHILE I'M GONE, Sally, you can keep up with your French studies right here." Thomas Jefferson slipped into the deep blue satin waistcoat which her brother held for him, then the dark gray woolen morning coat which Jimmy pulled from the mirrored wardrobe. "I've hired a tutor for both you and Jimmy. If the girls need help you'll be able to come to their rescue."

He turned and looked in the glass, checking the back of his hosiery clad leg. Sally supressed the smile that rose at his display of boyish vanity. Today he was wearing real shoes, the ones with the silver buckles.

"You look just right, Master Tom," Jimmy walked around the tall man. "Them foreigners gonna think you powerful big and handsome." Her brother winked at Sally as he plied his clothing brush. "But you'd look some better if you was to let me powder your hair."

"No powder, Jimmy. You know that. If they can't stand to see this red hair..." he turned to Sally, "Do you like the red hair, Sally? Do you think I should powder it or wear a wig?"

"I like the light on your head, Master. Do not powder it away." Sally let her dimples show for a second, then she put on a sober face. "We'll miss you sorely, sire."

"And I you," he held his hand out to her, "...all of you. Where are my other girls?" He pulled Sally toward himself then looked down into her eyes. "I will enjoy my trip through Holland and Germany much more if I know you will all miss me."

Sally nodded. She smiled her secret smile. "We shall all miss you. Will you be leaving tomorrow?"

"At the end of the week. I have a few items of business that must be attended before I go." He tugged her an inch closer to himself. "Can I depend upon you, Mistress Sally to see that my girls are well cared for? That my household maintains its serenity?"

"You need only give me your instructions," she slid her hand from the cage of his hand. "I will, with Jimmy's help, see that all is well here."

Jefferson frowned and cleared his throat.

"I wish to do something for you and your brother. You've been here for more than half a year now and Jimmy even longer. I have been remiss in a duty I have wished to take care of." He reached for her hand again and swung it with his own as if they were playing a child's game together and his gray eyes smiled at her. "While we are here in Europe I will pay you a wage for your work." He dropped her hand and glanced into the mirror again but he looked into Sally's reflected face rather than at his own. "We will start this week. Each Friday I will see that you receive a set sum." He cleared his throat again. "For the little things that you children need and want. I already do this for my girls, of course. You must not be without pocket money." His stare held her captive in the glass. "I want to show you how much I value you...both of you."

Jimmy pressed an elbow into Sally's side.

"Oh...yes. Thank you sir." She stepped back to allow Thomas Jefferson to stride from the room. "We'd both like that, Master Thomas."

"Tom, Sally." He smiled at her from the door.

"Thank you, Tom."

"Jimmy, you tell Israel what I've said. It is all arranged with him. He has your salary awaiting you."

"Yes sir!" Jimmy Hemings brushed against Jefferson in his race to leave the room. "Excuse me, sir."

"Now we are alone, Mistress Sally. May I have an early goodbye kiss?" He stepped back into the room and held out his arms.

She touched the satin charm beneath her fichu and glided toward him. Her other hand reached to stroke the satin of his waistcoat.

"Will you miss me, Sally?"

"Very much, Tom."

"Your face is a lovely flower, your ivory throat the columned stem from which it springs." His hands swept gently down each side of her throat. "See, child, your very presence causes me to burst into poetry."

Sally felt an almost unbearable longing to have those hands continue their caress down the length of her body. She stood still, submissive to his touch for a long moment. She lifted her face. He lowered his own.

His lips touched, pulled away, then touched again to press against hers, to open softly against her mouth. Sally hardly realized that her arms had circled the shoulders of the man. Her mouth seemed to flame with hunger for more of him and his tongue answered her longing. The kiss lasted a long moment, then another before he stood tall and laughed a shaky laugh.

"Ah, my little Sally. You are a womanly child, that is sure. Again. I want more."

Again they kissed and Sally felt as though her soul or her heart's promise or some velvety missive heavy with love had passed between them.

"Does Madame Cosway go with you on this trip, Thomas?"

"She does not. I go on a special survey for our government, alone, and I will be working, my darling girl. How I would love to have you as my companion."

"Then kiss me again. Perhaps that will keep me awaiting your return."

"I must guard against your innocence...and your guile." Again he bent to kiss her. Again she felt something pass between them. A signal, like unseen lightning, leapt the path between their lips and their intertwined arms.

Jefferson stepped back first.

"I must go."

"We will wait supper for you, sir?"

"Yes. Supper." He cleared his throat and he was gone.

The day seemed long to Sally. She did her schoolwork, and listened to Polly and Patsy. She gleefully counted the coins Jimmy poured into her apron, her wages. The first money she had ever had.

"You got more than I did, girl. What you gonna do with your money, Sally?" Jimmy's eyes held a far off look. As if he had suddenly been thrust into a new dimension. He tossed his coins from one hand to the other, then back again.

"I don't know. What will you do?"

"Maybe I save mine. Maybe I never go back to the little mountain."

Stay in France. Free. With some money of her own. She echoed the words Jimmy's dream called into her mind but another word intruded. France. Free. Alone.

"I'll think about it, Jimmy. It be different for you. You a man. I gotta think about what you say." She held a shining coin to the light. "Is it true what old Petit say, we free in Paris no matter what we are in

Virginia?"

"It's true, girl. Think of that!"

"I will, Jimmy. I promise." She smiled and made a jingling of the coins in her apron but she felt a spreading desolation inside herself, an emptiness that the clinking of her first money could not erase. "Wish they was some way we could get these pretties to mama, Jimmy. Wouldn't she be proud?"

Jimmy threw back his head and thrust out his chest.

"Maybe someday we bring Mama over here and show her then." His voice broke and he continued with a sheepish grin. "Petit say my voice gonna be sounding like a man's any day now."

"Are we grown up, Jimmy? Is that what happening to us?" Sally felt the touch of Thomas Jefferson's lips against hers and the flush of desire within the depths of herself. "Is that why we feeling strange? Feeling free?"

Jimmy's smile faded.

"You letting the master have his way with you, girl?"

"He kisses me. He calls me 'child'."

"You be careful, girl."

"Tell me what to do, Jimmy."

"I can't tell you what to do, Sally. Only tell you to be careful. Think what you doing."

Jimmy's smooth golden tan cheeks reddened under his sister's gaze.

"It different for a man," he explained, "We supposed to bed the willing girls."

"Jimmy! Have you...?"

"French girls. They like me." He winked and grinned, begging for understanding from his sister. "Say my French done be powerful pretty." He laughed aloud.

Sally stared at her brother. For a second she wished to be back in her linsey woolsey shift, back in the quarters with Jimmy and Critta and Mama and the others. Safe. With nothing changed.

Then she laughed, the sound strange to her own ears.

"Sometimes I wish I were a man. You're right, my brother. It different for a man."

IN THE KITCHEN Sally ordered the supper for the Master and herself and for Polly and Patsy. Petit emerged from the smokey recesses of the huge room.

"Ah, Mademoiselle. You have thought about what I told you?"

Sally nodded.

The little man took the tray from her hands and led the way up toward the dining room. He spoke to her over his shoulder.

"I would be most happy to show you the sights of Paris, Mademoiselle, if you wish."

"That's very kind of you, Monsieur Petit."

"Here, all are free. I think you like that, non?"

"Yes, I like that. Please don't speak so quickly, Monsieur. I don't yet understand as well as I should."

Petit pushed the door open with his back and let Sally move ahead of him into the hall. She saw Thomas Jefferson standing waiting in the dining room but she knew the Frenchman didn't see him. The man's next words were spoken more slowly and to Sally's ears they seemed to boom in the empty hallway.

"Mademoiselle Sally, you are what we Frenchmen call 'tres jolie.' Cheri, believe me, you needn't speak the language to be understood."

Silently, Thomas Jefferson walked to take the tray and motioned with his head for Petit to return below stairs. The littler man bowed and turned to go, but not before he sent a wide smile in Sally's direction.

"That man is getting above himself. If he did not come with the house I would..." Jefferson turned and stared at Sally, starting at her toes and moving upward, over flowered muslin and coffee dyed lace fichu, across her mouth, her hair, her cap of white linen. She made herself remain still, tranquil under his rage lit, searching gaze.

"Sally...have you been with a man?"

"I'm with you, sir. You're a man."

"No, no, girl. Don't play with me. You know very well what I mean. Has a man been in your bed already?"

Sally felt her face flame.

"No."

"Just 'no'?"

"I have been in no man's bed and no man has been in mine. I sleep in your youngest daughter's room as you know quite well. Who would be there with me?" The taste of gall was in her mouth. She must allow him any question, any demeaning conjecture about her character. He and he alone held her well being, her future, her very life in his hands. Sometimes the hands were tender, sometimes cruel. His eyes were the eyes of an eagle now. His crippled hand a talon.

A silent voice repeated the new idea within her. The word both

Jimmy and Petit had spoken.

"Freedom." But she didn't say it aloud.

"I want you to learn French quickly. I will send you to board with a French family while I am gone." He spoke in a whispered tirade of anger, "You are mine. I cannot, will not let you fall into the hands of..." His face blanched with heightened fury, "No. This is my decision. You will go to the country. You will go tomorrow. I will send word when you are to return."

Sally whirled without a word and left him standing at the head of his table. She brushed by Patsy, then Polly with her eyes averted, her bottom lip caught between her teeth. She forced herself to hold silent against the words that pressed and clamored to be spoken.

"I am free here, Thomas Jefferson. Don't you know that? In France I belong to no one except myself." The harsh sentences of banishment hissed at her heels and followed her like a snake slithering up the stairs behind her.

"Pack your belongings, Sally Hemings. Pack now. Tomorrow you go to the provinces. Away from Paris. Tomorrow you..."

She used both hands to slam the door on the snake's head.

Chapter 21

May 1788

WHEN, AFTER about four weeks with the Dupres she had begun to
dream in French, Sally knew she was almost mistress of the language.
The Dupre family, father, mother, the six children and the old
grandmother spoke not a word of English, so for more than five weeks
she had heard nothing but French morning, noon, and especially at
night since she slept in the bedroom with the three Dupre daughters.

Fifteen year old Claudine Dupre wanted to know everything about
Paris so their time after the candles were blown out was always spent in
feverishly whispered questions and uncertainly whispered answers
about the "city of light." The scent of smoke and candlewax drifted
through the darkness to become a part of their dreams of Paris.

The day the letter came, Sally was sitting on the side of their bed
trying to figure out what her recurring dream of ruined and broken
buildings had meant. Claudine's shout and the clatter of the girl's
wooden clogs against the stone floors of the Dupre farmhouse had
wakened her fully.

"Sally, a letter! For you! From Germany. Vite. Read it and tell me
everything it says!" The French girl shook the thick envelope above her
head as she ran.

Sally took the letter and turned it over and over in her hands.

"A letter. Just for me. From my master...from Monsieur Jefferson,
I think." She very carefully used her embroidery scissors to slit the
envelope open so that nothing on the outside was spoiled.

The thick sheaf of papers were in the familiar masculine
handwriting. "My dearest Sally;" she read aloud and glanced up at the
waiting Claudine.

"Claudine. May I please read it in private first? I promise to read
it to you as soon as I've finished. Do be a friend and let me read it to
myself first. I can read it quickly and translating is so slow. Come back
in half an hour, please?"

The peasant girl turned and left without a word. Sally knew she'd have to work to get Claudine into a good mood again but she didn't care. Having her own letter from Thomas was worth any amount of trouble.

She began again..."My dearest Sally..."

"In Dusseldorf I have really thought about you a great deal. A painting by the famous artist, Van der Werff, has effected me so much that I have gone again and again to see it.

"The picture is called 'Sarah Delivering Agar' and each time I see it I am thrilled anew. Perhaps you have not heard the story of Abraham's wife Sarah giving him a gift of a beautiful slave girl called Hagar because she, Sarah, could not give him a child.

"Hagar, that is,'Agar' in the painting, is traditionally thought of as the legendary mother of the Arab people. Van der Werff has painted her as a very young and innocently seductive girl of your age. Truthfully, she looks much like you, darling Sally. Abraham looks to be far from old...perhaps not much older than I.

"I cannot tell you how much this picture has been in my thoughts. I would agree to be in Abraham's place though the consequence would have been that I should have been dead five or six thousand years. I am, my darling Sally, loving what I see and feel, without being able to give a reason, nor caring much whether there be one."

Sally felt a thrill run through her as she read his words and she became even more excited at the last few sentences.

"You will be coming back to Paris, safe and sound, within the week when you read this. I have informed the Dupres and all is arranged. I have a gift for you my 'Agar.' I hesitate to say it but I must...I can only hope you will allow me to become your 'Abraham.'"

Crisp new franc notes had nestled within the sheaf of written pages. The money reminded Sally that now she had money of her own, that she could go about as others did with no worry about whether she would be required to pay or not. She could pay what was asked and even leave a coin or two under the pillows of Claudine's bed so the other girl could share in her good fortune.

Sally smiled at the thought of Claudine slipping her hand under the feather pillows to hang them out for the weekly airing of the bedding. The girl's fingers would find the centimes waiting there. A whole string of "Mon Dieus" would be murmured in that dark and smelly little bedroom, Sally imagined. Probably be the first money she ever own, too.

She thought about life on the Dupre farm then shook her head. This is not the way I want to live, she thought, not in some little closed-in house where even the mama works in the field like a horse. Monticello seems better, somehow...even the slave quarters seem better. Open. Sunny. The air freer. There was a flash from her childhood, a quick picture of herself and Patsy wildly racing their make belive horses across a meadow filled with wildflowers.

She shook her head. The Dupres and all the other French workers seem to live as if they're inside a closed fist. As if they're afraid of something.

The bone wrenching return trip in a public carriage seemed much shorter to Sally than had the same trip when she had been "banished" from Paris. She had hardly had time to pack her few belongings, say goodbye to the Dupres and now she sat in another hired hack outside the very door she had left so reluctantly weeks before.

She looked at the grime on her sleeves and hands, the dirt under her fingernails. Her hair felt sticky against her neck. A quick picture of the French maids pouring hot water into the tub in Polly's room made her smile with anticipation but she couldn't bring herself to step down to the paving stones. Would Thomas be there? Would the thing that hovered between them be resolved now?

And what about the present? The gift! Oh, the gift he'd promised. She'd almost forgotten. He'd said he was bringing her a gift. More silk for a dress? A bonnet? Ribbons?

"The only way you find out girl, is by going inside."

Stiffly, smelling of old sweat and unwashed hair, she stretched, then clenched her dirty hands into fists and stepped down from the carriage. She handed a coin to the coachman then hastened up the granite steps toward the huge front door. She raised the knocker and dropped it. After a deep breath she raised and dropped the lion's head again. She could hear the sound echoing inside the hallway, then footsteps coming to answer her demand for entry.

Through her dress and her light woolen pelisse she pressed the tiny secret satin bag hard against her breastbone. A special gift for his 'Agar?' What was it?

Soon, soon, all her questions would be answered.

Chapter 22

April 1789

THE DOOR SWUNG open to show Sally her brother's widely welcoming smile.

"Bet you a Frenchie now, for sure, girl." He embraced Sally with one arm and slammed the door shut with the other. "Oui, oui. You gonna come home talking just like one of them French girls, the Master say."

"Is Master Jefferson home already, James?"

"Came two days ago, now." His curious gaze meandered over her travel stained garb. "Bet first thing you wanting is a bath..." he glanced back down the hallway "...fore anybody see you." He swung her small trunk up on one shoulder. "Master he just take the little mistresses out to that there new museum. You grab your little portemanteau and let's just slip up the back way so's we don't run into anyone. You be looking like your usual self when they get home."

An hour later Sally felt herself smiling for no reason as she drifted down the front stair; face and body clean, hair clean and still wet from the bath and her clean dress floated gray voile over freshly starched and ironed white linen underskirts. Her skirts ruffled the scent of lavender into the air about her. That's one of the things I really missed at the Dupres, she thought, the chance to get clean all over.

The house was quiet and cool. At first the solitude seemed cleansing, also, but in another moment she felt a spurt of panic. The black and white checkerboard of the floor seemed to shift beneath her. It was as if she were in one of those strangely deserted buildings she's taken to dreaming of recently.

"Where is everyone?" First she whispered the words then she spoke them aloud but no one answered. She fingered the bag that hung at the cleft in her bosom. Other words rose unbidden to her lips. Words that held only the meanings and pictures of "home" and "Mama" and "Monticello" in her mind. But behind those pictures they held the old meanings, also. She chanted timeworn words. Words taught her by Betsy Hemings on long winter afternoons and through sultry summer nights. She bowed and her black slippers traced a row of invisible figures across the black and white marble floor. Her hands lifted and caught the tiny diamond shaped rays of light from the windows that flanked the entryway door.

As she danced James joined her in the hallway, he hurried to help by beating the old, old rhythms to lift her movements. He used the dark wood of the finishing arm of the balustrade as if it were a chest high drum...he pounded out the message to the African Gods. "Hear us, Chango," he called, his voice gutteral.

Sally whirled and hummed the same chant deep in her throat. She ended her dance two steps above the one where James stood, then poised herself in the last figure of supplication while smiling down at her brother.

"I want to see Mama and Critta and the others, don't you, brother?"

"I do, but I reckon I never will."

"Why not?"

"Me? I told you. I done decided. I'm going to stay here. Right over here. They love me over here. No chance someone going to send me down the river here." He left the balustrade to do a step of his own across the smooth black and white squares. "I dont told you all the girls like me here, little sister."

Sally swallowed the lump of sadness that threatened to overwhelm her joy.

"I want you home, brother, home with me. Mama want you home, too." She joined him on the shiny floor for one more sliding step. "I'll talk to the Master about you." She nodded her promise.

As they danced the door opened to flood the foyer with light. Brother and sister turned their faces to the entering Jeffersons.

"Oh, Sally," Patsy ran to embrace her, "I'm so glad you're home."

Polly too, shouted her own gladness and ran to clutch at Sally's smoothly pressed skirts. She crushed the white linen and gray voile into a rumpled ball of her own sweaty handed welcome.

"I thought you wasn't never coming back!"

"Weren't ever," Sally corrected the child automatically and put one arm about tall Patsy's shoulders and the other across Polly's back.

Patsy turned to the man in the doorway.

"See, Father. Sally's home. I said she'd be here."

"I'm happy to say that you were right, daughter." He held out a hand. "We missed you most terribly, Miss Sally. I believe this family needs you."

James glided silently away toward the kitchen stair and Sally sent a silent promise to precede him, then raised her hand to the outstretched hand of her Master. He bowed and let his lips touch the back of her hand.

"The Lowlands, nay, the rest of Europe, offered no artistry so fine as this first glimpse of our Mistress Sally." He straightened and continued to hold her hand. "We are, all three of us, most happy to welcome you home, 'Agar."

"Her name's Sally, papa," Polly corrected him.

"Yes indeed. Our Sally." he said and smiled down into her eyes. The silver gleam of his eyes' unspoken promise struck lightning into Sally's mind. A tremble shot through her and for support she pressed her hand onto Polly's shoulder.

"See, Patsy. Sally ain't never going to leave us. She's that glad to see us. Her hand's a shaking."

Thomas Jefferson nodded, glanced at the offending hand and smiled more widely.

Sally knew she was the only one in the room who could hear the sound of drums, the only one who could hear the throb of Chango's answering beat. Her mind recognized it as the charging of her own blood; her own blood drums pounding, singing, sounding the joy of the ancient invitation into her own ears.

She too, nodded.

ALL THROUGH THE long and leisurely late afternoon family tea, Sally was aware of her strangely heightened senses. The current buns seemed sweeter in her mouth, the steam from the teapot carried a fragrance more compelling than ever before. The blues and reds and greens in the carpet at their feet were almost painfully bright. The wrinkles in her gray voile overskirt appeared to lay a mysterious panorama of mountain tops and valleys across the starched white linen of her lap. Thomas Jefferson's silk clad legs stretched with delicious abandon into the center of their lazy circle. His hair glowed against the window's near twilight. His smiling gaze burned warm against her skin. She welcomed the diversion of Polly and Patsy's conversation.

"And Sally, old Petit has gone off somewhere and we like it better without him here, don't we, Patsy?"

Patsy nodded agreement. "Father sent him on some sort of extended errand, I think."

Jefferson's enticing laugh rumbled at the edge of their chitchat.

"And Sally, Papa says we can stay home and study with you and that we are going home to Virginia real soon."

Sally shot a questioning glance at the sprawling, comfortable man. He nodded affirmation. She felt her heart speed up. Home? Or maybe not. She must remember, now that the charm was set in motion, her choices on this day would affect the rest of her life.

She stole another glance at him. His gray gaze slowly traveled from her face to her feet then back again.

"Have I told you girls of the painting of Hagar and Abraham that I saw in Germany at the museum in Dussledorf?" He spoke to all of them, he looked at Sally.

"Tell us about it, Papa."

"Yes, father. You've mentioned it but do tell us all about it."

"We'd like to hear about it, Tom." Sally felt her heart speed a beat, "You mentioned it in your letter to me."

"It's a wonderful painting. Overwhelming, really, I thought. By an artist named Van der Werff. It tells the Bibical story of Hagar...and of Abraham in the most beautifully compelling way." His eyes never left Sally.

"Tell us what it showed, Papa." Polly stood by her father's chair then leaned against it. "Did you help paint it, Papa?"

Thomas Jefferson lifted his youngest to sit on his lap. "No, darling, I didn't help paint it but I wish I had. It was a great work that has had a most profound influence on me for the last several months."

"What's a 'profound influence?' "

Jefferson smiled down at the child. "That means I think about it a lot."

"Oh. Like the ship. And the Captain. And Aunt Eppes?"

"Something like that. Tell me darling child, are you still longing for your Captain and his ship?"

"Well, not so much anymore, I guess. I'm pretty happy now here with you," Polly smiled sheepishly. "I'm not scared of you like I used to be. I really like being here when we're all together."

"I feel the same way, Father." Patsy tapped her pale blue lace fan against the tea table. "Our house seems more...more...homelike when we're all four here together."

"When Sally is here, too?" he seemed to let his voice linger on the sound of her name.

"Of course."

"You're silly, Papa. Everything's more fun when Sally's here. You know that."

"I do know that. Thank you for reminding me, Mistress Polly."

Sally sat smiling, lids lowered, listening to the conversation. *He wants me to love him for himself. I could love him. Maybe I do love him...but I want more.* She refilled the cups around the small table. *What do I want?*

She gestured with the sugar bowl toward Jefferson. He shook his head "No" as did Patsy. Polly reached for the bowl but Sally shook her head.

"Only two lumps, Polly."

I want freedom and security for those I already love. His family is turning into my family but what about my other family...my blood family back home? What about Jimmy? What if I have a child? She touched the satin juujuu to remind herself. *I haven't chosen yet. I still have time.*

"...and when Sarah realized she was not going to have children," the cultured voice of the Virginian continued his story of the painting, "She knew she had to find another woman to cohabit with her husband. That was a faily common practice then, Polly. When a man took more than one wife they called the wives who came after the first wife, 'concubines' back then. Sarah looked for someone who could have the children Abraham longed for. She looked for a special concubine."

"Concubines," Polly murmured in her father's arms.

"Oh, Father, now she'll start using that word all the time. I'll be so embarassed."

Sally started to speak but stopped herself. *What would he say?*

"Now, Polly, 'concubine' is a perfectly good old word. You can find it in the Bible. But dear child, it's such a special word, with so much private meaning, that people don't speak it aloud in public. It's our secret word." He smiled at Patsy and Sally over the head of the eight year old.

"Oh. Like 'sod the old girl.' Right? I don't say that at school anymore."

"That's good darling. Yes. It's something like that."

Patsy heaved a sigh of relief.

"Thank Heavens. Go on about the painting, father."

"Van der Werff called the concubine 'Agar' but in our Bible she is called Hagar."

"Agar?" Polly whispered and looked at Sally. Sally gestured for the little girl and Polly left her father's lap to come and sit beside Sally.

"Well, in the picture, Hagar the Egyptian, was the concubine who was being given to Abraham. They were acting out their tableau in front of a beautiful bullseye window." He was silent for a moment. "Since she was of the Egyptian race she had the slightly dusky skin, you understand." He pointed at Sally, "She was just a shade darker than our Mistress Sally here. It is said that she became the mother of the Arab peoples. But she was beautiful, girls, gloriously beautiful, with long straight blonde hair flowing like a golden waterfall down her back."

Sally felt a small pang of envy. Blonde hair. She put up one hand to touch the piled mass of silky curls at her temple. Her hair was long, yes, but it was just ordinary old curly black hair. Agar was a blonde.

"Was she pretty as Sally?"

Before he answered Polly's question he took a moment to survey Sally. She sat up straight and lifted her head as she had seen slave women do in Virginia when being inspected by a potential master. She could almost hear Betsy Hemings' voice, "Buck up, girl. Only way you going to do any good is to look good."

"I have to admit...ah..." He paused. He's going to say that a house slave isn't like a beautiful woman in a picture, an Egyptian. With long blonde hair. Sally opened her eyes wide and stared defiantly at the man. He stared back at her for a moment then continued..." she reminded me greatly of our Sally."

Polly laughed and clapped her hands. "See Sally. That's why he called you 'Agar.' "

He cleared his throat. "Well..." and he paused again. Sally felt her heart stop. He's going to say that I'm not as pretty. "Comparing the two ladies," he chuckled low in his throat, "I'd say our Agar is the most beautiful."

"Yea-a-a-a."

Sally gulped back the sob that rose in her throat.

"Truly sir?" Her words were for him alone.

"Most truly, Mistress Sally. Your glorious black curls, your faultless ivory skin, your glowing dark eyes...and what painting could ever capture the beauty of the intelligence and life which flows through you?"

He spoke as if they were alone in the room. "You are a model of exotic loveliness." He pulled his gaze from her and looked in turn at each of his children, "Do you agree, daughters?"

"I agree," It was a shout from the youngest.

More slowly from the older, "Sally is very beautiful." Polly surveyed Sally very carefully. "Wonderful complexion. She is tiny and yet very womanly looking." To Sally, Polly's words sounded wistful.

"Now, Papa, she can be your concubine."

"Oh, Father. See what I told you? Now she's going to be using that word in every conversation." Patsy sighed.

Sally put her arm about Polly's shoulders and tugged the little girl toward her. Jefferson sat up straight and looked his youngest daughter in the eye.

"We wouldn't tell anyone outside our family but the word concubine means a woman who sleeps in your father's bedroom. In my bedroom. In my bed. What would you say to that, Mistress Polly?"

Chapter 23

August 1788

"COME CLOSER to the fire, little one. August is a beautiful month in Paris, but sometimes cool." He gestured toward the warmth of the hearth. "At least I find it cool when it rains. Especially at night."

Sally slipped closer to the small blaze in the library fireplace. Now she stood almost touching her master's knees. Standing, she was nearly eye-to-eye with the seated man. She kept her gaze down.She smiled. Jefferson's silk clad feet were thrust into the beloved, old carpet slippers. Sally felt a small twitch of relief. Somehow the slippers made being together in this room seem ordinary, everyday. But she knew nothing was ordinary. Nothing was everyday. What happened here would, most likely, mould her life. She had to get it right.

Her fingers sought out the tiny satin bag that hung about her neck. That work had been done. Now she must see what could be done about her future.

Jefferson's hand followed hers and brushed against the gray voile of her sleeve.

"Ah, Mistress Sally. Perhaps we should be thinking of new clothes for you. Polly's castoffs are very pretty on you but every young girl wants something new. Am I right?" His hand continued to move down her arm. "New dresses. Gloves. Bonnets. Perhaps a bangle or two?" He raised his hand to lift her chin. "Shall we make a list of what is needed?"

He's not asking about clothing, Sally followed his moving hand through the heat that his fingers traced upon her arm. He's really asking me to agree to what is already fact. He owns me. But he knows I'm free here, if I choose. And it's not just that. He wants me to choose to be owned. Shall I choose that? James says he can take care of both of us as a chef, now. Can I stay here with my brother and live as a free woman?

"James says we are free here in Paris." The words came involuntarily and the angry flash of his eyes frightened her but more

words tumbled out. "James says he can work here and take care of me."
She felt her breathing deepen. "Perhaps I can work also." Now she'd
done it. The words were said.

Jefferson stepped to the bell cord and pullled it. A frown creased
between his eyebrows. His lips were tight against his rage. She knew
he'd sounded the bell to call for James. He returned to his chair in front
of the fire and he reached to take her hands in his. He took a deep
breath.

"Perhaps James is not telling you everything."

Sally opened her mouth to speak but Jefferson placed a finger
across her lips.

"Wait until your brother tells me all these things he has been
telling you...then you and I will talk."

What had she done? Were her words going to make trouble for
James? How would he answer the Master's questions? How could he
answer without angering Jefferson further? The Master's red hair
glowed in the firelight, his freckled skin flushed. He looked young,
angry, determined. Sally wished it were daylight so she could see his
gray eyes more clearly.

When James appeared at the door he glanced at her before he
spoke to Jefferson. He was smiling but wary.

"Yes sir, Master. What can I do for you?"

"You can tell me what you've been telling your sister. You've
been filling her head with fairy tales of working and living in Paris."

James rolled his eyes at Sally. She could see him struggle to
answer. He stood silent for a long heated moment, then he seemed to
relax. He straightened his shoulders as if he'd made a decision.

"Just talking with my little sister, master. Making plans. Yes sir."

"Yes sir, what?"

James darted his browneyed glance toward Sally and she nodded.
He bobbed his head twice. Sally knew the look on his face. A white line
appeared from his nose to the corner of his lips on either side of his
mouth. James was furious, too. With her, she wondered? No. Maybe
angry that he had to share their secret before they'd made any real
plans. Her brother took another deep breath.

"I done told her I be going to get me a chef job here in Paris. Petit
say he help me." The strange smile on James' face was unreadable. "I
just been telling Sally I help her if she want to stay here with me when
youall go." He took another deep breath. "Ain't it true you planning to
go back to Virginia, soon, master?"

"You both belong to me!" Somehow Jefferson's words seemed to ring with pain. A light glowed behind Sally's eyes. It was as if a candle had been moved more closely to her face. That was it. He knew they could be free but he didn't want them to know that. He wanted both of them to choose to stay with him, to choose to be his slaves. "I give you both a salary, now. Why would you want to go as a cook to any other house?"

James stood silent for another long moment. When he spoke his voice didn't break but it deepened with the emotions that gleamed from his eyes. Nearly eighteen now. He's a man grown, Sally realized.

"Well, just being practical, Master Jeff, I could make me a lot more as a chef," he emphasized the French term, "...than you been paying me." He paused. "Fancy chef, again the emphasis, "Gets big money in these Frenchies' kitchens." He balled one hand in the skirt of the linen apron he wore. "These here folks values their food." James smiled at Sally but she read his dark glance. He had thought about this and he knew what he was saying. "Ever'body want to be free, Master Jefferson,...even slaves. But you know that."

"James, I don't want to lose you." The older man turned his face up as if he were looking at James but he slewed his gaze toward Sally, "Either of you. Maybe a little raise?" He stood with his back to the fire. He was a broad shouldered, slim hipped silhouette looming over her and her brother. Sally couldn't read his face. "Let's talk about this some more but you be thinking about this. I could take you home and you could be freed there...legally"

James grunted a laugh that spoke disbelief.

Jefferson continued, his tone gentled as it did when he spoke to his horse before mounting, "To set you two loose in this society would be the cruelest thing I could do to you." He put his good hand on Sally's shoulder. "Why you two would be like children turned out into a strange, dark forest among the ravening wolves."

She looked from Jefferson to her brother James. He had her mother's light coffee with cream skin color. The older man's skin was white sprinkled with pale brown freckles. Red blotches on his neck revealed his anger. James was younger but he wasn't as large as Thomas Jefferson. Both looked fit and strong. She loved both of them in different ways. She was drawn to her master's red and white and gold coloring. He be an elegant man of the world, she thought, James be younger, and handsome but reckless with his life, maybe with mine?

Jefferson's hand clasping her shoulder burned itself into the skin and sinew and bone of her. She lifted her fingers to touch the man's hand but she let hers drop. She felt a moment of decision speeding toward each of them. Let it come. His pain was not yet her pain. Her comfort was not yet his comfort.

"I just about made up my mind, Master Jeff. I was just waiting to the right time to tell you."

"What about your mother? Your other brothers and sisters? You'll never see any of them again."

Sally knew Jefferson's words were meant for her as well as for James.

"And home? You'd be happy knowing you'd never see the 'little mountain' again?"

"Monticello's your home, Master Jeff. Ain't none of mine."

"You'll have to speak French for the rest of your life. The whole idea is absurd. Illegal."

"Legal in France, Master. And I ain't afraid of French. My grandmammy, she give up her African language along with her freedom. I can sure give up English and get some of that freedom back." He grunted the strange laugh again, "And iffen Sally stay here, she be my tie with home and family and speaking English. It'll all work out. You'll see."

James has more courage than I do, she thought, he's a lot like mama. He knows how to stand up for what he wants.

"I can't let Sally go." The words rang in the air above Sally's head.

"I tell you Master Jeff, she free here. She go with me iffen she want to and they ain't nothing you can do about it."

Sally felt as if she should scream her own words...but what words? They were bartering her as if she weren't in the room with them.

"Stop it, both of you." Her whisper froze the two men in their angry tableau. In seconds they both spoke to her.

"What you want to do, girl? You better decide."

"Sally, I love you. Don't leave me."

"You love me?" Again her words were whispered. Tom too, had a reckless courage. He'd let his most private feelings be made public. She wondered if she could have made the declaration had she been him.

"Yes. I do love you. I want you with me."

"James, couldn't we work something out with the Master? Mama be so sad if you stay in Paris."

"Come, shake hands, my boy." Jefferson held out his right hand.

"I will pay you an additional...twenty francs per month, James...and..." He looked down into Sally's eyes. "If Sally stays with me I will pay her more also." James ignored the outstretched hand. Jefferson's cheeks flushed but he said no more.

"You promise you'll give James his papers if he goes home with us, Tom?"

Jefferson nodded.

"Oh, James. Maybe this is the answer." She put her right arm through Jefferson's and her left through her brother's. "Mama will never forgive me if I leave you behind."

"You a choosing him, Sally girl?"

"Yes, James. I guess I am." She heard Jefferson's quick intake of breath.

Sally understood the smile James gave her. It was almost as if he'd said, "I'm doing this for you." He kept silent another moment.

"I'll stay, Master Jeff." They walked together toward the library door. "I do it with the understanding you gonna give me my papers back in Virginia...and you gonna be good to my little sister, Master Jeff."

"You have my absolute promise on that."

When James had gone Jefferson lifted her with his good hand to press her against his chest as if he were holding a child. She circled his neck with her right arm. His shoulders and his chest were a plateau of warmth and strength to Sally. She leaned toward him to let her black curls rest against his gray satin waistcoat. She could feel an embroidered silk fleur-de-lis against her cheek.

"Tom," she murmured.

He bent his head to kiss her gently, carefully, softly. Again, it was almost as if he were kissing a child. She liked being cared for but she felt confused. Why was she feeling like an infant? Sally let her other arm creep up to encircle his neck. She opened her mouth against his. Their kiss deepened and the touch of his lips against hers promised untold sweetness.

She was a child no longer. The choice had been made.

Chapter 24

TAKING TWO STEPS at a time in a smoothly athletic motion, Thomas carried her from the study up to the top of the stairs. She let herself again lean into the gray satin waistcoat. At the top when he looked down into her face she smiled up into the silver glint of his compelling gaze. Her mother had been right all along. Betsy had told her how it would be. It felt wonderful to have the decision made, to know that this man was her destiny. She felt safe. Secure. Whatever happened from now on, she was in his hands.

She stiffened. What was that? It was as if Betsy had spoken inside her head. She couldn't just let her future fall entirely into someone else's keeping. She couldn't just let that happen. She must not fall into the pattern of letting every decision be his.

"Tom. Let me down. I'll go the rest of the way on my own." He continued toward his bedchamber. "Thomas." She punched him in the chest. "Let me down this instant." Her tone brooked no argument. Time for some training. Let him learn that she was a woman who knew her own mind.

Puzzlement written on his face, he loosened his embrace and let her body slide closely against his own to allow her feet to touch the carpet. Color rose in his face then receded, leaving his skin paler than ever. The usually light freckles stood out against his white skin.

"What's wrong, my little Sally?"

"I'll walk into our sleeping chamber on my own, my love. I'm a grown woman now." She glanced up at him with a smile. "I've chosen this arrangement, Thomas...on my own. Let you remember that." His silver gaze darkened. She could see herself in his eyes.

She stepped into the bedroom ahead of him then turned and curtsied then offered him a gesture of entry and welcome. He smiled and came through the door. His shoulder length hair was caught at the back of his neck with a black ribbon. Somehow it seemed more pleasing to her that his hair had not been newly powdered that day. She liked the glints of red that the firelight sparked from among the previously whitened strands.

"You are so beautiful, my glorious Sally." he murmured. "More beautiful even than Hagar in the portrait."

He still doesn't think of me as a real person, not as a woman grown, she thought. He has some kind of thing he be playing out in his head with this Hagar woman in that picture he always talks about. She smiled up at him. Better let him learn that Sally Heming was real.

"Tom?"

He smiled at her whisper.

"Yes."

"Thomas Jefferson."

He smiled again.

"Yes, my darling Sally?"

"Are you going to kiss me?"

He led her toward a chair. He sat down and positioned her to stand between his knees. He stared at her before he reached to pull her closer to him.

"Yes. I'm going to kiss you. I'm going to love you. I'm going to make you my very own, Mistress Sally."

"I already belong to you."

"No, not the way I wish you to belong to me. But you will, my darling, you will." He glanced at the bed.

"You misunderstand me, also, Thomas. I am not talking as your 'slave.' I'm saying I've chosen you because I've loved you for so long. Since I was a child." Something flickered in the gray gaze. Yes. He was seeing her, Sally Heming, not some slave child he could order about, not some woman in a painting in a gallery. Now he was truly looking at her. He drew her even closer.

"Have you loved me, Mistress Sally? Even before this?"

She nodded in solemn triumph.

"I've always loved you." She felt his hands tighten. "I always knew we would someday be bound to each other." She was pleased that he returned her smile and even more pleased that his own smile was shy, and a bit tremulous. "Even my mother knew." She remembered how silly Critta had thought she was because she wouldn't sneak off with the boys the way Critta and the other girls did.

He ran his good hand up and down her arm.

"I don't want to frighten you, dearest. I will be very careful of you."

"Then you must kiss me, Tom. Is not that the way lovers begin?"

She felt glad she'd waited for this man. Offering him her virginity would bind him to her with bands of iron her mother had told her.

"Oh, yes." He pulled her to him and his lips against hers were gentle. She could feel his breath quicken. The kiss deepened. She wrapped her arms around his shoulders. He held her as closely as he could, one hand on her back, the other smoothed down her back.

"Open your lips, darling." He breathed the words into her mouth as he kissed her.

She allowed his tongue entry. She felt herself go faint, let her bones melt against this big gentle man. She could feel the hard muscles in his back and shoulder move under her hands. Closer, yet more closely, they each tasted and laved the mouth of the other.

Sally's eyes closed of their own accord. The whole world centered right here, here with this man's mouth upon hers. Strange feelings radiated from the center of her being into every part of her body. She wanted to stay this way forever.

"Let us move closer to the fire." He stood and helped her move nearer the hearth. "The night is chilly." He whispered the words as he untied her white linen half apron and cast it aside. He lifted the gray fichu from about her shoulders. "Will you be afraid if I undress you?"

She shook her head but remained silent.

"I want to look at every part of you."

She herself lifted the tiny satin bag from between her breasts then pulled it up and over her head to toss it to lie upon the voile collar and the linen apron. Her mother's teachings were waiting to be put to use. She could do without the charm and he could do as he wished with her. She had agreed to this. She had no more will of her own. Her breasts, her belly, her inner being, longed for Thomas Jefferson's touch. She felt proud that he wanted to see her body. She wanted him to love what he saw.

THE GOLDEN FLAMES in the fireplace leaped higher for a moment, to send heat and shadows dancing against her ivory skin. In the firelight she could see that her nipples had darkened and hardened on the pale globes of her breasts. She watched his eyes trace the indentation of her tiny waist and then move lower to look at the silken darkness that curled in the vee below her flat belly.

"You are miniature perfection, Mistress Sally." His voice was husky, almost inaudible.

She turned slowly, guided by his hands, slowly, slowly, as if mesmerized. She still felt dazzled by the silvery search of his gaze. When her back was to him he removed the pins from her hair and loosened the mass of satiny black curls that hung almost to her waist.

"You are perfect, perfect, from every vantage point, little one." Again she felt the words more than heard them.

"Will I frighten you if I too, remove my garments?"

She pivoted to face him. Without answering she began unbuttoning his gray satin waistcoat. He stepped out of his old carpet slippers without looking down, then shrugged out of his vest. She smiled to see that the homey old houseshoes had been the first things to go.

He lifted both of her slender hands to his lips and kissed the tips of her fingers before he finished disrobing. For long moments they stared at each other.

He so tall and muscular. Strong. White skin, freckled on every part of his arms and shoulders where he'd long worked in the sun, building and carrying for the construction of each new addition to his beloved Monticello. The maleness of him rose from a nest of red-gold hair.

She, so small, but lushly proportioned. A woman, rounded and firm. Skin like ivory on her face and hands, as white as he on the whole of the rest of her body. She was all creamy silk disturbed by only one tiny dark mole at the beginning of the mound of her right breast. He touched her there with his good hand.

"My Hagar." He whispered the words.

"No. Your Sally, Thomas, your real Sally Heming. I'm flesh and blood. See me before you."

"Your beauty mark." He bent and kissed the small brown circle. "Now mine."

She shivered. She didn't think she could stand it much longer if he didn't take her breast in his hand. She felt a desperate longing to be touched, to be held, to be kissed, by this man whom she had long known was her destiny.

"Oh. You're cold." He led her to the bed and lifted the cover to allow her to lie back upon the white linen sheets. She lifted her arms.

"Come into the bed with me, Thomas."

He lay down beside her and pulled the bedcovers up over the two of them. He lifted himself to one elbow so he could look down at her. His body radiated a delicious heat. He bent to claim her mouth with quick, teasing kisses.

She closed her eyes and took a deep breath. He smelled lightly of woodsmoke and the French cologne Israel patted on his face after he'd shaved the master. There was something else...a trace of musk, the very masculine fragrance that was the scent of Thomas Jefferson and no other. She closed her eyes but she could still feel him such a vital, strong presence looming above her. Her heart pounded. He was life, her life from now on. He was what was real.

He'd propped himself on his whole arm. He had not yet touched her with the withered hand. She reached for his wounded fingers and drew them to her breast. She heard his smothered gasp. Oh. Of course. He was still worried that she would be repulsed by his imperfections.

"Thomas, when I said I loved you, I meant all of you. Let us have no secrets, no holding back." She arched against his hand begging him to take more, to do more.

He pulled her into his embrace and kissed her fully. Their little universe between the soft covers became a heated paradise, a velvet cocoon for both of them. His hands working up and down her back aroused wild desire within her. When he cupped her buttocks in both hands she wanted to cry out with the sheer joy she felt. He buried his face in her neck and murmured all the things she'd longed to hear from him.

"I love you, Sally."

He also whispered warnings.

"I will try not to hurt you, my darling." She clutched him to her to say without words that she didn't care what might happen. She only knew she had to have him inside her.

"There may be pain at first." She arched and pulled him into her, her own need for him overcoming his hesitancy. The hurt was over in a second and she forgot it in the joy she felt. She opened her eyes once to the flickering darkness and firelight but she couldn't keep them open. She let herself be taken. She followed his lead and lifted to his thrusts. Quickly, then more quickly. She wanted more, more, more, until an explosion of sweetness, of fire, shook her. Waves of joy engulfed her. She shuddered and she was up and over the edge. He too, climaxed at that moment. They clung to each other, breathless and silent for a moment, staring at each other in wonder before he fell to her side panting. She turned so they faced each other. She searched his face for answers and she realized he searched hers for the same reasons.

"Was it...?"

"Was I...?"

"Did I hurt you?"

"Oh, no. Only for a second. A good hurt. Oh, Thomas. You're wonderful. That, that was..."

He pulled her close and chuckled.

"That, as you call it, can only get better, my lovely little darling." He took a quick breath. "That was only the beginning for us." He brushed a kiss on each corner of her mouth. "We have our lives ahead of us." As he spoke she could feel his manhood rising against her leg once again.

The second time was slow and easy, as if the two of them danced to some unheard music. The melody lasted a long time and later they agreed, each with the other in the age old way of lovers. They smiled and agreed that the second time had been even better than the first. Then they pledged in whispered declarations that every time they loved each other, the lovemaking would get better and better. Forever and ever.

Chapter 25

April 1789

SALLY SMILED AS she smoothed the white woven coverlet over the bed to which she and Thomas retired each night. It had been more than two weeks now, and she still felt the same delight she'd felt that first night. It had seemed strange to her that on their second night together Thomas had asked her to do up the bed herself rather than leaving it to the French maid.

"I just don't want strangers touching our secret place," had been his explanation and she'd been making the bed every day since.

"Oh." She put her hand to her mouth. Something in the dinner last evening had not agreed with her. They'd always tried to have a special dinner on the weekends when Patsy and Polly were able to come home from the convent school. She'd been nervous about what the girls were thinking...about all her new clothes, about her sleeping in the master's bedroom. She closed her eyes and smiled. It was obvious that their father could not keep his eyes nor his hands off her...even when he and she were in the company of his two daughters.

Sally brushed the small worry aside. Polly was no problem and surely Thomas could handle Patsy. She felt nausea rise in her throat. She poured a drink of water from the pitcher and the seasick feeling subsided before she'd taken more than a swallow.

She straightened and took a deep breath to make herself as tall as possible and walked to the glass to adjust her new bonnet and her new pelisse. Today they were going out to the shops to get gloves and ribbons and lace and boots and all the things that could not easily be made at home. Sally ran her hand across the black silk braid on the jacket. All the new clothes had taken hours for the fittings but she'd not objected to even one moment of the boredom of standing still for the dressmaker. She was looking like a woman, now, a woman of substance, Thomas said.

No one would ever take her for a countrybred slave. Not now. She twirled and looked at herself over her shoulder. Stylish. He loved the way she looked, Thomas said. Maybe while they were out today they'd get the two gold wrist bangles he'd been promising. She turned and looked once again at the front of the dove gray woolen dress and pelisse. The black silk braid trim was just the right touch she thought. Young, and stylish and dashing, Thomas had said.

She felt the growing eagerness to see him welling within her, the same eagerness she felt every day now. It was wonderful to have him all to herself most of the time. Except for the few times when Patsy and Polly were allowed to leave the school she didn't even have to concern herself about his two daughters. She had him all to herself. She controlled her impatience so she could make herself appear to "float" down the stairs in the proper manner.

She desperately wanted to run but she was quite aware that Thomas would think such behavior "childlike." He'd caught her racing Polly down the stairs the week before and had given them both a lecture on "ladylike behavior." She smiled at the memory and at what had come after. He'd wanted her to go back to the bedroom with him as soon as Polly had disappeared from sight down the hallway. Of course she had gone back up the stairs with him. With pleasure. His fierce hunger for her was no greater than her own for him.

She scratched lightly at the library door, then entered. Thomas Jefferson smiled at her over the letter he was reading. Sally felt a harsh spurt of anger at the sight of the tiny writing covering the page he held. She remembered the things Martha had once told her about her father's love affair with Madame Cosway. Both girls had been afraid he would make the woman their stepmother.

"You've received another letter from Madame Cosway?"

He nodded and let the paper flutter to the desk as if it had burned his fingers.

"You've continued to write to that woman?"

Jefferson's face hardened slightly.

"I have."

"Why?"

"We discuss many things...philosopical questions and political ideas mostly. Why do you ask?" The gray eyes were sharp metal that pierced her own.

"Careful," The voice of her mother spoke in her ear, "A jealous sounding woman ain't never gonna get what she wants out of life."

"No reason, darling. I was just surprised." Sally moved closer to the desk. "It must be wonderful to be able to discuss such things with a man like you."

The metallic frost left the gray eyes.

"A man like me?" He caught her hand in his good hand and pulled her closer to him. "What do you mean, dashing Sally, when you say 'a man like you?'"

She lifted his hand to her face and pressed her cheek against it. She let her voice go to a longing whisper.

"So famous all over the world, so important to the American government, so educated. I just know there is no other man like you, my darling Thomas Jefferson." She widened her gaze and looked at him, her mouth a pouting "O" of concern. "Who could blame Mrs. Maria Cosway for her interest in you, master of my life?"

"Do you really think me so special?" The gray eyes were lit with a smile now.

"You are special...to the whole world, to Polly and Martha, but especially to me, Thomas. You're more special to me than anyone has ever been."

"Ah," He bent his newly powdered head to brush his cheek against hers. The acrid scent of the blanc dust rose in the air. "My darling Sally."

He straightened and she leaned against him. She lifted the letter covered with the tiny feminine handwriting, then let the paper drift back to the desk.

"Oh, if only I were able to discuss philosophical questions and share political ideas with you as Madame Cosway does." She lowered her voice and gave a wistful sigh. "That really is my greatest desire, my love. To be educated enough to converse freely with you."

He put his hand under her chin and lifted her face toward his own, his gray eyes dark with love.

"You're a little minx, Sally." His lips descended. "Impudent lass." She closed her eyes to better feel his mouth on hers. She'd learned that kissing was such a lovely thing to do. She wanted every kiss he wished to give her. His lips felt warm and dry against her lips, then he opened his mouth as did she. His kiss still made strange thrills trace their way across the lower part of her belly. She'd never tire of the love she'd chosen, she knew.

After a long kiss he drew back.

"Shall I give you books to read so we can discuss what is going on in the world as well as other things that interest me? They might interest you as well."

Sally nodded.

"And would it displease you if I told Madame Cosway that I could not continue our correspondence?"

He smiled.

"That would certainly not displease me, sir." Sally flashed her dimple. "I believe just the opposite. I believe it would please me."

"Then let it be so." He pulled a fresh sheet of paper toward himself and lifted the quill from the ink stand. "I will write such a letter this moment."

Sally put her hand over his hand that held the quill. "Are you sure, Thomas?"

"Kiss me again and I will be," He chuckled. "I believe I have one of the smartest women in the country right here in my house and in my bed. I will educate her." He again gently chucked her under the chin with the edge of his thumb. "What do I need with a cold-hearted European widow?"

Sally smiled and lifted her hands to the back of his neck to meet the second kiss he offered. She felt a twinge of pity for Maria Cosway but that emotion lasted only a fleeting second to be replaced by the joy his words aroused. She was intelligent and now perhaps she would be truly educated. Why not, with such a magnificent tutor? Perhaps she could make herself less envious of Patsy and Polly when they chattered about what they were learning and what the nuns said and how strict the classes were.

She made a silent vow. If she ever had a daughter she'd teach the child how to read before she taught her anything else. Sally's hungry mind yearned toward the infinite world of learning which had just been offered to her. She could hardly wait.

"I'll soon be able to talk about anything you wish, Thomas. Just wait. You'll see." Her stomach roiled slightly and with an effort she quelled the upset. "Last night's back-to-school pheasant for the girls apparently didn't sit well with me. I think I'll just have me a tiny bit of tea and toast while you have your breakfast, darling."

Thomas Jefferson finished the short letter, sanded it, folded it and placed it in a heavy brown leather pouch before he rose to take her hand. He stepped back and let his gaze take stock of every part of her appearance.

"Even tea and toast with you, would be a celebration, Mistress Sally. Come. I'll join you, then we'll be off to the shops to search for the little gold pretties I promised. I'm none too hungry myself." He bowed and lifted her fingers to his lips. "You look quite, quite beautiful this morning, my little love." His smile broadened. "If last night's pheasant didn't suit, something must be coming right for you. You're positively glowing."

WHEN THEY returned from the shops their carriage brimmed with packages both small and large. The two gold bangles were not in any one of them but were resting in cool splendor on Sally's wrist. Thomas smiled when she purposely jangled the two of them and held out her arm to admire the shining gold.

At the top of the steps, Jefferson's male secretary met them with a letter. Sally knew at a glance that the missive was from Martha. She knew that handwriting very well. Patsy's awkwardly shaped letters had changed very little from the days they had all studied together.

Jefferson slipped the note into his coat pocket as he directed the emptying of the loaded coach. Upstairs, in their suite, after everyone had bowed their way out, he opened the envelope as Sally began an inventory of admiration for all their purchases.

His grunt of anger alerted her.

"What is it, Tom dearest?"

He held the letter out to her, his face pale, the lines grim. The freckles stood out in bold relief against the white of his skin.

"Mistress Martha tells me she wants to become a nun. Wants to retire to a convent."

"Patsy?" She took the sheet of paper and glanced at it.

"Yes. This turn of events would give great satisfaction to my enemies, not to mention the papal nuncio."

"But Patsy hated the nuns when we were at school together. She thought they were tyrants."

"Well, you can see what she has written. This is a formal request for permission to become one with them. A 'bride of christ' no less."

"You're not even a Catholic."

"Nor is my daughter. She is doing this for quite another reason than religion, Sally." His eyes were silver embers of anger. His gaze wandered over the disorder of packets and paper on the bed. Sally read the hidden message.

"My fault." The words sang silently in her blood. "Somehow this is all my fault." Sally lowered her lids and looked once more at the jumble of ribbons and lace before her. Martha couldn't stand to live in a house where a slave slept with her father, where a young slave girl was loved and honored by her father.

"Martha was my best friend when we were children." Sally backed a step away from him. She wanted him to say she wasn't to blame.

"I do not believe she feels the same way about you now, Mistress Sally." His voice was rueful, the words steel. "I'll think about this. We will talk again." His lips thinned in a mirthless smile. "I am quite determined that my daughter will never become a nun hidden away in a French nunnery." He turned. "Never." He repeated the word before he left the room.

Sally perched on the edge of the bed. The gold bangles felt cold against her skin.

Within two days Jefferson asked her to sleep in Polly's room for the next day or two.

"Permanently?" Sally could barely make her voice be heard.

"No, oh no, my little Sally." He turned her to face the looking glass, then embraced her from behind. "Are we not a handsome couple?" His arms tightened about her. "See how well you fit my embrace?" He smiled at her unsmiling reflection. "I wish only to make peace with my family then all will be well again." He bent to kiss her just behind her ear then he whispered. "I will never let you go, my own. Never." He had rolled up the sleeves of his white linen shirt and the hairs on his arms glinted golden red in the glass.

On their first morning home, Polly told Sally what had happened when her father had shown up at the school.

Jefferson's carriage had rolled up to the door of the abby, all the little French nuns whispering and bustling about as he strode into the reception room and asked for the mother superior. Jefferson had a short private conversation with the Abbess and moments later his two daughters stepped into his carriage to roll toward home, their baggage to follow, their school days over.

Polly repeated all the details at breakfast the morning after they'd returned home. Sally had felt such loneliness because she was back in Polly's room. She missed him. She missed him terribly. Neither Martha nor Thomas Jefferson joined them at their meal.

"I'm glad I don't have to go to that bloody school anymore," was all Polly had to say after she'd retold the story. "I'd rather study here with you, anyway, Sally. I don't care what Patsy says about you."

"Watch your language, Polly." Sally hardly heard her own automatic words. What was Martha saying? Now the girls were to be living at home what would happen? Were she and Thomas once again to be forced into secrecy? Maybe he'd put them into another school. If only she and Thomas could be married, that would solve all their problems. Even a jealous daughter could not complain about a father who slept with his wife, could she?

Sally excused herself to the nine-year-old and slipped away from the breakfast table. She barely made it to the retiring room in time to bend over the nearest chamber pot. The small piece of cod and the slice of buttered toast she'd eaten, made their way back out of her belly and up and out through lips they'd entered only moments before.

"That stupid pheasant. I can't seem to get rid of these cramps. I'll ask Petit for something to settle my innards." She murmured the words to herself in the nearby mirror as she sat in a chair and dabbed at her mouth with her linen handkerchief. She closed her eyes and tried to recover from the waves of sickness that had just shaken her. She gave herself orders. "Girl, you can't afford to be sick like this now, not with him so angry and upset."

That day Martha ate all her meals in her room. Jefferson maintained an outward calm and a smooth demeanor.

"Our Patsy needs a day or two to recover from her disappointment," he explained and that was all he said about her.

That night after dinner and after Polly had climbed the stairs toward her bed, Jefferson asked Sally to return to "their little nest," which she did and their joining was as wonderful as before...except for the fact that his two daughters were back in the house for good. She lay staring into the darkness long after he slept. What was going to happen next? She could only wonder. She felt as if the house and everything and everybody in it were simply waiting, poised for something, she didn't know what.

Chapter 26

May 1789

SALLY SWUNG her legs over the side of the bed. She stretched her arms above her head and for a split second the musical sound of the two gold bracelets tinkling against each other diverted her. In an instant her smile died and she dropped her hands and sprinted across the floor to dive behind the modesty screen so she could stand over the chamber pot once more, her inner being trying to tear itself out of her and up through her throat.

"Oh, God." She retched again until only greenish liquid poured up through her mouth. "Sick. So sick." She staggered back to the unmade bed and threw herself across it. The linen sheets felt clammy with her sweat.

Polly stuck her head in the door.

"What's wrong? You sick?" The youngster stepped into the room. "Father says he wants you to come on down to the breakfast room."

Sally could only groan.

"Eeew." Polly put her hand over her nose. "You're kind of smelly in here, Sally. You won't want Father to see you like this, I suppose. You want me to send the housekeeper or Martha or someone up to see about you?"

Not Martha. With effort, Sally turned her face toward the child. She could certainly smell herself. Every part of her body felt sticky. No wonder that the nine-year-old wrinkled her nose. The whole room smelled of vomit. Oh, God. She'd promised Polly a walk in the park today after their lessons. Sally desperately wanted to stand up and say that nothing was wrong but when she lifted her head she had to let it fall back against the twisted sheets and she could only groan. She could see fear rise in Polly's eyes.

"I'll tell my father you're ill, shall I?"

Sally nodded but she was afraid to speak, afraid the heaving churning inside of her would start once again. She closed her eyes and let herself relax into the protection of the feather tick. If she could just lie still a little while with her eyes closed she might live. If she could go back to sleep she might rid herself of this vile sickness. Whatever it was. This morning's bout of nausea had been the worst yet.

She drifted and dozed for several minutes before she heard someone else open the chamber door and step inside the room. Please God, not Thomas. She didn't want him to see her like this.

"You sick, little sister?"

"Oh. Jimmy. You're not supposed to be up here." She couldn't make herself sit up. Her brother stood at the side of the bed staring down at her. "Thomas don't want none of the servants but me in here." Her words were a croak.

"Fuck old Thomas. You sick, girl. I come to see about you." He put his hand on her forehead. "He down there eating and talking with them Frenchy politicians. Them two dutiful daughters is doing a little polite embroidery in the drawing room. And I come up here to see about my little sister."

Her brother's tan skinned hand felt so cool and comforting on her forehead that she couldn't seem to control the tears that rolled down her face. It was almost as if her mother were touching her. It felt like home and childhood. Betsy Heming shared a satin smooth cafe avec creme skin color with her son Jimmy. He looked like mama, too. When she was little she had wished she could trade her pale skin for the smooth buttery tan covering her mama and her brother wore. Sally knew she was going to die and that Jimmy was the only one who truly cared. He'd tell her mother what had happened to her. Helpless tears rose in her eyes. She'd be buried in this foreign country. She'd never see Betsy Heming's beautiful tan mother's face again.

"He be mad if he find you here." She was too sick to watch and edit her speech. She forced the plantation patterned words out in a dry whisper. Once again her stomach rebelled at her movement.

"I don't care 'bout him, Sally. What's wrong with you?"

"I don't know, Jimmy. I think the pheasant was bad last week and I been real sick and a getting sicker ever since." Her stomach roiled. "Throwing up my innards." She scurried toward the chamber pot behind the three panel screen. Nothing came up.

Jimmy was grinning when she fell back onto the bed.

"You not sick, girl."

"If I'm not sick why do I feel so bad?" She opened one eye to peer up at her brother's smiling face. She closed her eye at once to slow the room's tilting whirl.

"You acting just like Mama did when she carrying you. She was servicing old John Wayles then. Maybe that had something to do with it. Maybe white babies make you sicker. The babies she had with old Wayles made her real dizzy. She was like to vomit up her heels every morning. Almost couldn't work." He patted Sally's shoulder. "And she was worst when she carried you." He chuckled. "Ain't nothing wrong with you but something purely natural. You having a baby, Sally." He tapped her flat belly. "You with child. You pregnant."

"Pregnant!" Sally shot up in the bed then raced again for the chamber pot. She heaved but nothing came up. She stepped out to look at him. She wiped her mouth with the back of her hand and stared at her brother. "You think?"

He sat on the edge of the bed and nodded solemnly.

"Pregnant?" She whispered the words. "I've conceived?"

Jimmy nodded once more as she joined him on the side of the tousled bed. He put an arm around her shoulders.

"Looks like you gone and done it, little Sally."

"What am I gonna do?" She felt a storm of emotions at war inside her. Delight, fear, anger, worry, contentment, joy, puzzlement, grief. She felt them all. "What will Thomas say?"

"What can he say? Maybe he say 'Congratulations Sally dearest, for making some new little slaves for me and my plantation?'"

Sally tried to shove him from his perch on the side of their bed but she was too weak to move him.

"My children ain't never gonna be slaves."

"Honey, they's slaves iffen they mother is slaves. Now that's one thing I do know something about. In France they's free and back in Virginia they is slaves." He tightened his embrace for a moment before he stood. "Maybe we better have us another talk with old Master Thomas Jefferson. Maybe you and me better stay in Paris?"

"Oh, Jimmy. We made him a promise."

"Oh, well then. We sure as hell wouldn't want to break no promise to old Tom, not even to save our children being slaves." Jimmy disappeared behind the screen where she could hear him pouring water from the pitcher. He emerged with a dampened linen towel and brought it to the bed to bathe his sister's face. "That be what you saying Sally girl?"

LATER IN THE day, when Sally felt more herself, she dressed

carefully, choosing a pale green muslin that Thomas especially liked. She pinched her cheeks for color, then descended the stairs, one hand touching the banister. She felt the need for care. She was no longer nauseated but she felt as if her legs were empty reeds tottering on her new French slippers with the high heels.

At the library door she stood silent for a moment, took a deep breath to compose herself, then scratched for entry. She stetched one foot forward to look at her new shoe but even the glimpse of one of the shining silver shoe buckles that Thomas had chosen for her couldn't seem to cheer her. She'd loved them when he'd given them to her, now the ornament didn't seem to matter. What was he going to think? What was he going to do? She straightened and scratched again. No answer. She stepped inside the library with no invitation.

The room was empty but it was apparent that Thomas Jefferson had just stepped away from the desk. The morning's mail lay fanned out across the polished wooden desktop as if he had emptied the bag in a hurry. Among all the other letters were three from Madame Cosway. Sally couldn't bring herself to sneak a peak at the letters themselves but she stacked the three perfumed envelopes in a neat pile at the corner of the desk. That way he'd understand that she knew he was still receiving mail from Maria Cosway.

When she stepped back into the hallway Jefferson was strolling down the hallway toward her.

"Ah, Mistress Sally," Jefferson smiled broadly, then frowned. "This has been quite a day. I hardly know what to think. Should I be happy or sorry? He stood staring down at her. "What think you?"

Sally eased into one of the chairs that flanked the library door.

"You've already heard?" Her voice broke on the last word. What a disappointment. She'd wanted to tell him herself.

"Yes. Well, I've had no official notification but some people in the know brought word today. I think Madison will be sending a letter soon." He moved to stand beside the chair where she sat. "I've wanted it and I've dreaded it. Now I can't help being excited." He absently lifted one of her black curls and let it circle his finger. "Perhaps you have something to say on the subject?"

Madison? A letter?

"You've heard about it already, Tom?"

"Well, yes. The men who came today let the secret out."

"What are you talking about, Thomas?"

"Going home, of course, my dear." He pulled her to her feet.

"Madison wants me to become a part of his new government. We may all soon return to our beloved Monticello, dashing Sally. And about time! Perhaps we'll leave within this very month. Would you like that?"

Chapter 27

Late August 1789

SALLY SLOWLY REGAINED consciousness to find she was lying cradled within Thomas Jefferson's strong arms. She realized she must have fainted.

"What happened?" She stared up into his face. Anxiety made his eyes dark as gray storm clouds against his white face. Was he worried about her? The odor of the powdre blanc drifted in the air where he held her and she wrinkled her nose. "Tom, I like your hair so much better when you don't put that stuff on it." She put her hand across her face to protect herself against the scent. "Just the trace of that dusty smell in the air makes my stomach turn over."

His face stiffened and he released her to let her feet touch the floor. Oh, now I've hurt his manly pride, she thought.

"I'm sorry I seem so malodorous to you, my dear."

Oh, he was too sensitive by far. Still it was up to her to humor him. She'd better watch her mouth no matter how she might feel. She laid her head against his chest and clasped him close with both arms.

"I have something to tell you, Thomas."

"Besides the fact that I make you sick?"

"Tom, Tom. It isn't you that makes me sick...well, in a way I guess it was you...Oh, Tom." She tugged on his hand to guide him to the chair against the wall where she'd been sitting.

"I'm so confused." She gently forced him to sit so she could stand between his knees and look into his eyes. She stared at him in silence for just a second then smiled.

"I think I'm going to have a baby. Our baby. My brother explained everything to me." She searched Jefferson's face for a reaction. "That's why I been so sick at my stomach, Jimmy says." His face was carved in frowning stone. "Mama was the same way, he says." Still no reaction. "I'll be fine in a week or two, Jimmy says." What was he thinking? "I'll feel wonderful, Jimmy says, just like mama did when she carried me."

She couldn't read the unsmiling mask before her. "Oh, I hope it's a boy, don't you?" she leaned toward him. All energy left her. The smartly high heeled slippers seemed unwilling to hold her upright. She wilted against his chest again. She could hear his heart pounding.

"A child?"

She tried to read his feelings in the sound of the two words.

"Yes."

"Are you sure?"

"Jimmy says he's sure."

"Hadn't we two better be the ones who make sure?" He held her shoulders to put space between them so he could look into her eyes. "Perhaps we should call a doctor."

"Whatever you think best, Thomas." Sally lowered her gaze and for a moment she let her long eyelashes rest against her cheeks before she again looked up at his unsmiling face. Her heart sank. His silvery metallic eyes screened his thoughts from her. He was very unhappy with her news. She just knew it. She drew a shuddering breath that was close to a sob then whirled from him to run back up the stairs to their room. Their bed, she told herself, was the only place where she could feel secure.

His voice pierced the clatter of her racing heels tapping against the marble.

"Sally. Wait."

She ran on.

"Sally. I'm sorry, I didn't mean..."

She slammed their bedroom door to close her ears against the rest of his words. He wasn't really sorry. Not the kind of sorry she wanted from him. He was sorry she was going to have his baby. That's all. That's the only kind of sorry he was. She threw herself across the bed.

Racked by sobs of disappointment she pounded her fists against the feather mattress until she was so tired she could no longer cry. Still he didn't come. She sat up on the side of the bed.

"You better think, girl," she said aloud, "Think what you gonna do, now. Better think about yourself." She stood and kicked off the new shoes and stripped off the silk stockings she'd been so proud of earlier. She planted her bare feet against the coolness of the polished wood before she began to pace about the room. "Better think about your baby." She spoke the last words through gritted teeth. She'd talk to Jimmy again...and to Petit. They'd help her do the right thing. Sure. They'd help her plan. She stepped to the door, peered out and listened.

No one around.

She slipped out and headed toward the shadowy back stairway that led down to the kitchen. Mr. Thomas Jefferson would never think to look there. Her smile was bitter, her feet cool against the narrow wooden steps that led down to the belly of the house. Only servants and slaves were ever seen on this set of stairs or in the kitchen, of course. Never, never, the Master of the house nor any of his family.

AFTER A LONG discussion with Jimmy and a few minutes with Petit, Sally again used the back stair to return to the bedroom. She had made her decision.

She went directly to the box she'd shoved into a corner of the room, a box of her things from "before," things she no longer wore or used.

With nerveless hands she lifted the lid. She stood staring down for a second as if she'd forgotten what she was looking for then she knelt and began to dig through the contents. Her fingers scrabbled through the linsey woolsey and cotton and linen garments unable to hold onto things. Maddened, she felt as if someone or something pressured her, hurried her, pushed her against her will.

"Stop it!" she said aloud to force herself to pay attention. "Think." Thomas would come in at any moment she was sure. She had to be ready. She plunged her hands to the bottom of each back corner and patted and pushed and searched for what she wanted.

Where was it? Stupid to let something so important get lost like this.

Her right hand finally closed around the tiny satin bag. She breathed a sigh of relief and grasped the juju tightly to pull it to the surface of the twisted and confused clutter in the box.

She could hardly control the trembling as she lifted the bag and the string that held it. She let the string drop about her neck like a necklace then she settled the satin juju bag into the cleft between her breasts, both necklace and bag hidden by the pale green fischu of her dress. She let the wooden box lid bang down before she raced to the mirror. She touched the charm through the green cloth and smiled at her reflection before she said the words her mother had taught her. In her mind she could see Betsy Heming as she'd looked on the last day before they'd left for France.

Sally pressed both hands against her still flat belly and spoke.

"Now, baby, my tiny baby, now you are protected. I'm your

mama. I will take care of you and keep you well. Don't worry." She felt a small jolt, as if her hands had recieved an answer from the growing child. She looked at herself in wonder. "Why...my baby knows I'm taking care of it!"

She heard the doorknob turn and she walked unhurriedly to perch on the side of the bed, face composed, fingers of one hand touching the satin bag, the other touching the place where the baby lay.

Thomas Jefferson walked into the room and stepped aside to allow entry to a short stout Frenchman carrying a small leather bag.

"Mistress Sally, this is Monsieur, uh, Docteur, Dupre." He gestured toward the little man who nodded at her. "I would like you to let the doctor talk with you, darling, perhaps examine you, and then we will know for sure whether you are really with child or not." His last few words were deep in his throat and somewhat strangled. "I've told him you speak French." Jefferson turned and left the room then opened the door to look in again. "I'll be right outside, my dear."

WHEN THE DOCTOR had finished, nodded at her and stepped out into the hallway, Sally again invoked the powers that had been the special gift of her mama. The two male voices talked on and on and then silence.

Jefferson stepped back into the room.

"Well. Doctor Dupre says he thinks you to be enciente."

"I know, Tom. I told you I was."

"Best to make sure my dear."

Sally let her gaze lock with his.

"What are we going to do, Tom?"

"Everything will be all right, my dear. You have my word on it." His gaze dropped and his last words were muffled in his white linen cravat. "I will see that everything is taken care of, you can be sure."

"What does that mean?"

"Just that we must do what is best."

Sally stared at him, anger choking her. "You mean you want to have our baby killed, don't you?" Her words quavered and ended with a sob.

"It would be much the best solution, all things considered, darling." He put out his hand and patted her shoulder as if to sooth a recalcitrant horse. "Don't you agree?"

"No. I don't agree. And you are not considering all things." She jerked away from his touch and stood. "You're not considering me.

You're not considering my feelings. You're not considering our baby. You're wanting to kill our love."

"Please don't pace about, Sally dear. Let us discuss this together in a more civilized manner."

"Please Master Jefferson," She let the tears flood her cheeks, "Remember I ain't civilized. I'm just a slave." She raised her skirt. "See. I'm just a barefoot nigger girl walking around on your fancy floor." She let the skirt drop. "Why discuss this with me, anyways, sirrah? You already done made up your high and mighty white man mind."

"Oh, Sally. Sally my love." He took a step toward her.

"Don't you come near me." She picked up a porcelain shepherdess that stood on the bureau beside her. She examined the blonde haired, blue eyed figurine for an instant. "Bet you think this here thing looks like high and mighty white lady Madame Maria Cosway." She laughed through her sobs and aimed the pretty china thing at Jefferson's head.

He threw one arm up and ducked. The statue crashed against the wall behind him and shattered into a million shards of fired clay. Both stared first at the broken figure then at each other. Sally giggled and he chuckled.

"My dashing Sally. Oh, how I love you."

He took her into his arms and fell onto the bed, still holding her, still laughing.

"Life is never dull with you around, my darling." His face sobered and his lips touched hers. Their kiss lengthed and deepened. His hand moved to her breast. His touch was heated against the tenderness she felt, as if the breast were swollen or bruised. She wanted his touch even though her nipples were sensitive almost beyond bearing.

She remembered the time she'd bruised her heel as a child and then was unable to keep from touching the bruise even though the touch had pained her. She'd even liked the hurt that had felt good. When the bruise had healed she'd missed it. This feeling was much like that had been.

"Why are you smiling, my little Sally?"

"I was thinking that my breast feels something like the stone bruise I had when I first came to Monticello."

"Oh, am I hurting you?" He lifted his hand.

"No, no." She pulled his hand to her breast again. "I love the feel of your hand on me."

"You were such a beautiful little girl."

"Why Tom, you never even looked at me until I came to Paris."

"Oh, but I did. I knew even then that you'd be a beauty someday...and I was right." He lifted a strand of her hair and curled it around his wrist. He smiled and bent toward her.

They kissed.

"Liar. But I love you for it. I hate to think about life without you, Thomas."

"Madame. I do not lie." He raised his hand as if taking an oath. "I swear by this sweet breast that I did truly watch you grow up and that I always noted your charm and your grace and your beauty."

She giggled.

"Liar."

"No. Now let me see." He allowed her dark curl of hair to fall from his wrist then he let his hand absently tweak the waiting nipple. "I believe your stick horse was named...Brummell, uh, no, Bunell... uh...Bucephus. Yes, that was it. Bucephus. Many times I watched you gallop him up the wide drive and tether him to the colonnade that my study overlooked."

Sally felt a prick of surprise. He really had been noticing her...even when she was a child. Her blood heated and she pulled him more closely to herself. She let herself search his handsome features as if she were seeking some kind of secret pleasure that only he could provide.

"Turn over, Thomas," she whispered, "Let me ride my Bucephus once again."

"OH MY GOD, Sally. You are extraordinary." He groaned and looked down at her. "I never believed that lovemaking could be so wonderful as it has been with you." He fell to her side, stretched full length against the rumpled sheets. "Having you has made my life worth living once again. I love you, darling."

"I love you, too, Thomas." She stared silently at the plasterwork cupids that decorated each corner of the bedroom ceiling. "All the cupids watched us." She pointed. "Wasn't Cupid also called Eros, the God of Love?" She looked at his relaxed face. "This room is perfect for love, isn't it?"

He opened his eyes and followed her gaze. He focused, then smiled.

"Cupids, by Jove." He sat up in the bed. "Sally darling, you're right. I'd never paid them much attention. I'm afraid I just took them to be French angels or religious figures of some sort." He leaned to kiss her on the cheek. "Of course, any room would be perfect for love if you were in it. I'll prove that when we return to the little mountain."

Sally sat up also and swung her legs over the side of the bed to sit next to him. She let her hand rest on his thigh. She silently compared the skin on their bare legs. Hers like ivory, his almost blue white like marble. She wondered what the baby's skin would be like.

Thomas loved her and she loved him but the problem still hadn't been solved. But she'd made up her mind. She'd just have to broach the subject again. Something had to be decided. Today. Or as soon as she could arrange it.

"Tom, we could get married in France. I asked someone about it." She looked at his face in a sideways glance. "You could tell people in America that we met in France. Mama and the others wouldn't say anything to anybody."

The shock on his face caused her stomach to clench. Jimmy and Petit had been right. "Ain't never going to marry you, girl." Jimmy had said. "Not in this world." So. Marriage was out of the question. He'd already dismissed that idea. Not even to be discussed, apparently.

"You know what I promised Martha, Sally. On her deathbed, too. That I would never remarry?" He stood and walked to the window, his strong white back to her. "You remember surely?" His muscles bunched and rippled in a show of negation. "No, no, darling. Marriage isn't an answer for us." He looked back over his shoulder then moved to begin dressing. "I'll think of something. Don't worry."

"Your wife Martha was my sister. Did you remember that, Tom?"

He turned to stare, his face shocked.

"Well, yes. I did know. I'd forgotten."

"It's all right to have relatives who are your slaves but we woudn't want to marry one is what youall believe?"

"Oh, my God, Sally." His words were a shocked murmur.

"I'm not killing my baby."

"I know. I know." He hurried to shrug into his ivory satin vest. She knew he just couldn't wait to get away from her, from their room, from this predicament.

"Thomas. We have to talk about this." She grabbed his dove colored waistcoat and held it behind her and backed away from him. "We can't just close our eyes to the fact that I'm going to have a baby."

"I said I'd think of something." the note of irritation was back in his voice. "Give my the coat now, dear. We'll talk later."

"Tom, I have to know now." She backed another step away from him. "What will happen to my child? Our child? Will he, or she, be a slave back in Virginia?"

Jefferson froze in place. His face went white. His eyes hardened to slate. His mouth became just a grim line.

"Well? Will he? Be a slave?"

"I don't know. I don't know." His voice cracked as if he were almost crying.

She felt pity rush through her but she forced it back. She couldn't weaken on this. Jimmy had warned her that she was too softhearted.

"Oh, Tom, a slave." She could say nothing else.

"I daresay. What else can the child be? A well treated slave has not such a bad life." He reached for the coat. "Isn't that so?" He smiled his public smile. "We don't have to decide now."

"I've decided." She glared at him and once again hid the coat behind herself. "I know exactly what to do."

"Come, come, Sally. I must get to work." He again reached for the coat. "I've a great many papers to go through. The diplomatic pouch arrived earlier."

"I know." She nodded. "I glanced into your study."

"Well, darling, I must go."

"No, Tom. Listen to me."

"What is it?" He sighed.

"I must take back my promise. I cannot go back to Virginia with you. Neither Jimmy nor I can go." She lowered her gaze. "I'm sorry, Thomas."

Again he froze. Staring. His eyes gray ice.

"Not go back with me. What are you saying? You promised."

"Things have changed, Thomas. You must listen." She shook his arm. "Our baby is not going to be a slave. Jimmy and me and the baby...we'll live in France. We could live free here."

"You'd stay here...in France...without me?" His face turned ashen and he sank again to the bed. "You'd part from me so easily as that?"

"I wouldn't part easily, Tom. I love you, but I must think of my child. The only answers you've given me are 'kill him,' or 'forget about him,' or 'make him a slave.' None of those answers suit me so I shall have to find another answer, another way." She allowed her own features to harden with decision. "A lifetime of slavery is not something good to look forward to...and I want my child to have something good in his future."

Jefferson bent forward, his elbow resting on his knee, his forehead resting in his hand. His voice was bleak.

"I think I cannot live without you, Sally."

"Will you give my child his freedom?"

"What would a child do? Even if he were free where would he go?"

"He can live with us until he is, uh...until he is...uh...twenty one. Then you can give him papers and a little money and let him make his own way."

"And if it's a girl?"

"The same. "

"Even for a girl?"

"Most especially if it's a girl." Sally placed protective hands across her belly. "Girls need even more help that boys do." She looked down at her hands. "I've noticed, Thomas, that girls aren't allowed much freedom...even white girls that are legally born free into good families."

Shock rode his face.

"What are you saying?"

She raised her gaze to meet Jefferson's.

"Look at poor Polly and Patsy. They can't step one foot out of the house unless someone is with them." Sudden realization of the circumscribed lives that young women led flooded Sally's consciousness. "Why here in France, I have more liberty than the two of them do...and I'm a slave."

"Stop saying that, for God's sake."

"Isn't that what I am, Master Jefferson?"

"No! Uh..well," Jefferson cleared his throat. "You're in a very important position in this household. I love you. My children love you. The servants all respect you...and...and..."

"And I'm a slave."

"Mistress Sally," His words were forced out over lips set in a grim, stiff line. "You recieve a salary in return for any work you do here."

"Would I be getting wages if we were in Virginia? Living at Monticello?"

"Why are we still discussing this, Sally?"

"I need to know my real, my legal position, Jimmy says. Petit says so, too." She picked up the green muslin and let it drop over her head. She left her fischu and the crinoline and the petticoats where they'd landed in a heap on the wooden floor.

Jefferson put his hand to his forehead as it he were in pain.

"I'm afraid I'm in for one of my headaches."

"I'm sorry, Thomas." He really doesn't want to think about this but he must...even if I have to force him to do so. He has to pay for his pleasures, just like Jimmy said. "I know your headaches are terrible but escaping into one of your megrims won't solve anything." She reached to touch the side of his forehead with a lightly sympathetic caress. "Our problems will still be here. They'll still have to be talked about."

He nodded but said nothing and he didn't look at her.

"In particular, Thomas, we must decide what we're going to do to guarantee some kind of a good life for our child."

"We'll talk more of this later." He slid into the waiting carpet slippers then grabbed his waistcoat and as he struggled to put it on he left the room.

"We surely will, sir." She called after him.

He shook the powdered red gold of his hair and waved his good hand against the air as if an insect were bothering him, but he didn't look back.

"Well," she murmured, "Going to be up to me just like Jimmy done said." and she headed for the backstairs.

Chapter 28

"WELL, YOU WANTED an *avocat*. I brought you one." Jimmy shoved a scared looking, thin man ahead of himself into the kitchen. The skimpy gray hair on the man's head waved about in the air, like weeds growing from a rocky patch of ground. His neck seemed swollen. Scrofulous creature, Sally thought, but what do I care if he can do what I want.

Petit slipped in behind Jimmy. "Petit here found him." Petit giggled and moved closer to Sally. Jimmy gave him a dark look and he moved away from her.

"I done told you, Petit. *Laisse ma soeur tranquille*! Stay away from my sister. She's not for you." He grinned at the French valet. "Old Master'll have you for dinner, boy, should he find you sniffing around Sally."

"Sniffing? Mais non!" Petit frowned. "What is this 'sniffing' mean?"

Jimmy shrugged and ignored his friend to look at Sally and point with his thumb at the skinny, wild haired newcomer.

"Your avocat, little sister."

"Avocat? Oh, yes, lawyer." Sally held a sheaf of papers against her stomach. "I wrote all this in English. Do you think he can understand?"

"I'll explain anything that you can't, little sister." He gestured to the puzzled looking stranger. "He talks a little English. His name is Monsieur Marceau. Let's sit here at the table and we can get all your stuff written out." He repeated his words in French and the man smiled and sat at the long table where the servants of the house usually had their meals.

"Can he notarize the paper when it's finished?"

"Sure. These here French lawyers can do it all, Petit say."

The four people huddled at the well scrubbed table for several hours until they were asked to move so the cook could put out the servants' evening supper. They scooped up the papers and moved them to Jimmy's bed.

After another few minutes in the room that Jimmy shared with Petit, Sally felt satisfied that they had covered all the problems that might rise in the life of her baby. She nodded and Avocat Marceau dripped an impressively large dollop of wax onto a folded tricolor ribbon which he had placed at the bottom of the paper. He then pressed his silver seal into the wax to fix the ribbon in place. Afterward he scrawled his name and his position.

"Looks mighty important." Jimmy held the paper up to squint at it.

"It is important, Jimmy. This paper holds my baby's future." She locked her gaze with that of her brother. "If Thomas don't agree then we just got to stay here in France. You still willing?"

"More than ever." Jimmy handed the lawyer two coins." I thought we was making a big mistake going back, anyways, girl." He shrugged again as if he had said all he was going to say.

THAT NIGHT SALLY chose one of her new evening gowns, a creamy rose colored silk dress dripping with delicate cream colored, handmade lace. Thomas had chosen the dress so she knew he'd like it. It seemed a bit too fancy for dinner at home but Sally knew she probably hadn't much more time that she could wear the garment.

Patsy would probably hate it. Anyway, better get the good out of it right now. She put the folded paper into her matching lace trimmed reticule and leaned toward the looking glass to pinch color into her cheeks. With her movement the new bangles made golden music together.

Fine.

She would have to handle this very, very carefully. She touched the ornate gold locket Thomas had given her while she was still at school, then she smoothed the small satin bag that rested below it. The locket rested on the outside of her garment, the satin juju against the special place between her breasts under the lace fischu. Her mouth moved with the words that would make all go right if she kept her wits about her. After the silent chant she smiled at her image and turned to leave.

She waited at the first landing until she heard the scuffing of slippers in the hall below. He'd already dressed for dinner. He'd probably used Jimmy's room to change to a black waistcoat and crisp white linen but he'd kept the old carpet slippers. His long beautiful legs were sheathed in white silk to show them off but the foot at the end of each of the elegantly shapley masculine legs was firmly settled into a worn woolen scuff. She had to smile at that. The fact that his vanity could never win over his desire for comfort was always so endearing to her.

She knew Thomas loved seeing her floating down the stairs. He'd told her more than once that it always made him want to take her right back up and into the bed. That will come later, she promised herself and she started her slow descent.

"Shall we go into dinner together, Thomas?" She let her voice flute lightly into the air above his head.

He smiled and the smile faded as he watched her walk down the stairs. She had his full attention. She could see that his eyes were smokey with desire, almost as if he were seeing her for the first time. Sally touched the charm lightly and returned his stare with a look that promised him everything. "Shall we go in together, sir?"

"We shall." He extended one arm and she placed her hand upon it. "Your new gown is most becoming, Mistress Sally."

"Thank you, kind sir." She gave him a sidelong glance. "It is a recent gift from an admirer."

"Clever man." He smiled widely. "I'm sure Patsy and Polly will be most impressed."

"Darling...I've been meaning to tell you...Patsy wants us to call her Martha at all times, now. She's very set on that." She tapped his arm with her ivory fan. "We must do as she says. After all she's a young woman, now."

He nodded solemnly.

"Martha it is, Mistress Sally." He seated her at the foot of the table. He smiled at his daughters, one at each side of the table. "Sally has reminded me that you must now be called by your real name at all times, Miss Martha. I will endeavor to remember to do so." He bowed and smiled at his oldest on his way to the head of table.

"I still want to be called Polly!"

Sally nodded and looked at the youngest.

"And so you shall be, Polly dear."

"How come you're so dressed up tonight, Sally?" Polly craned her neck the better to see the creamy rose silk and lace panniers that billowed out at each side of Sally's chair. "You look kinda like a princess."

"Quit being so silly, Polly." Martha firmed her lips into a straight line and looked down at her own hastily chosen gray muslin dinner gown. She turned her gray eyes to stare at her father. "Father thinks young girls should dress simply, don't you father?"

Jefferson had to tear his gaze from the rosy vision seated at the end of the table in order to give his eldest daughter's question his attention.

"Oh. Yes of course. Right, right, Martha. Simplicity is very becoming to young girls." He lifted his wine glass to Sally. "However, I believe our Mistress Sally may be celebrating something tonight."

Oh, my God. He's going to tell them about the baby tonight. Sally looked down at her hands.

"What? What?" Polly's voice rose in excitement. "Are you going to marry my papa, Sally? Will you be..."

"Don't be such a childish idiot, darling sister," Martha's icy voice cut into Polly's questions. "Father can't marry Sally. She's just a slave."

"You're right, Martha," Sally touched the tiny satin charm before she smiled cooly at the older girl. "And no, Polly." Her smile for the younger girl was real. "Your father and I are not getting married." She turned the dinner table conversation toward Polly's day. As Polly burbled on about her walk in the park, Sally stole a glance at Thomas and she realized that the frown line had returned to the usual space between his eyes.

LATER, IN THEIR bed chamber upstairs, Sally dipped and swayed and hummed her own accompaniment in a private dance around Thomas Jefferson.

"You're in a very good mood, tonight, Mistress Sally." He loosened his linen neckcloth as he talked.

"I am." She twinkled and twirled then lifted her skirt a few inches to allow him a glimpse of her silk clad ankle. "I think I have solved our problem, kind sir."

"You may have solved one problem but you're causing another, darling girl." Jefferson shrugged out of his coat, then loosened his satin knickers. "However, this problem can be easily solved if you'll just come on over to the bed with me."

"First, I want you to take off all your clothing, Thomas, and get yourself into the bed." She held up the lace trimmed reticule. "Then I'll finish the show for you." She curtsied deeply, eyes downcast. She lay the reticule down and snuffed the candle on the dressing table, leaving only one flickering flame on the table beside the bed.

"Oh, in that case I'll hurry. Don't want to hold up Terpsichore."

He tore off his waistcoat, his shirt, then his hose, and tossed all aside as if they were no more than rags. "See," He jumped into the bed, punched up the pillows behind his back and gave his full attention to her performance.

Sally removed the silken panniers and hung them in their place with the other hoops. She danced each article of clothing to its proper place. In moments she stood in her silk shift, her silk hose and her new high heeled slippers with the silver buckles. She lifted the shift to drop it into the corner then rescued her reticule from the dressing table. She continued her sensuous movements clad only in her silken stockings and her high heels; the tiny bag of magic resting between her breasts. She could see the reflections of the candle flame in the silver buckles on her feet.

She let the silver chain of the lace reticule dangle from her fingers allowing the little purse to play its part in the intricately patterned movements of seduction. Her shadow mimicked her every gesture on the wall behind her.

"Mistress Sally," His voice was hoarse. "I don't know if I can stand this much longer."

She could see his rising manhood outlined beneath the sheet. She stood silently and looked directly at him and waited. She listened for the words that always came when she needed them.

"Do this right and you'll save your child." The voice in her head always seemed to be that of her mother. Sally nodded and opened the reticule to bring out the folded parchment.

She whirled the reticule and let it fly to land in the corner of the room atop his discarded smallclothes.

He sat up a bit straighter.

"What do you have there?"

"The answer, darling Thomas." She swooped and swayed and flashed the French lawyer's seal. "This is an agreement twixt the two of us." She raised both hands high in the air and let her body sway toward him, then away from him in a series of intricate movements.

"Written by a lawyer. Tells what we going to do, my Thomas."

She turned her back and bent to let her ivory buttocks entice him, meanwhile, slowly fanning her backside with the heavy paper. She wiggled backward toward him, then rose to her toes to twirl in place, the paper flaring in the air.

"My God, Sally. You're killing me."

One arm in the air holding the precious paper, she slithered about the wooden post at the end of the bed as if it were a huge dildo. She smiled over her shoulder and winked at him. She could see the spear of his need lift the linen sheet even higher.

"You going to let my baby go, Thomas. Let our baby go. Let him live free when he's grown."

"Anything you want, my darling Sally. Now come here." He grabbed for her but she danced away from the bed just inches beyond the long arm's reach.

"Educated and hard working and free, my baby can do whatever he wants." She swayed toward the other bedpost and kissed it slowly, sensuously, as she wrapped one silk clad leg around it. She arched backward, the paper held out in a fluttering dance of its own. "Once his daddy signs this here paper, my baby boy Jefferson can do anything he want."

Jefferson again reached for her.

"If he is anything at all like his mother, he can rule the world." Jefferson chuckled and pulled her into the bed.

Chapter 29

October 1789

THE LURCHING carriage seemed to be taking forever. Sally wrapped her arms around the mound of her belly as if to protect the one soon to be born.

"Never mind," she whispered to the kicking child within her. "We'll soon be at home, soon be at Monticello. Soon see your grandmother." She raised her head to lean from the vehicle. Would they ever finally, truly be there?

The wagons and carriages and boats and ships and carriages again, had seemed to want to jolt her to death before they would ever reach their last stop on their neverending journey. Her heart leaped. There it was. They could look upward toward the brick mansion. Already Jefferson had tapped the roof of the vehicle to stop their carriage. The vehicles following stopped as well.

Jefferson stepped out, as did Polly and Martha. Jimmy and Petit and the other servants stepped down from their wagon also. Sally stayed in the carriage but stared out the window to look up as all the others were doing.

Their angle of travel gave them a clear view of the facade of the beautifully sited house. Sally caught her breath, impressed for the first time by the beauty of the place. When she'd left it the place had simply been "home," now she saw that it was a mansion that was more beautiful than many of the European residences she'd seen.

Graceful, the pedimented portico eyecatching, the entire facade was perfectly balanced. Built of red brick finished with white trim, the whole structure sat waiting like a colorful jewel set out upon the golden green velvet of a Virginia autumn lawn.

"100,000 bricks," Jefferson said the words like a song or a chant, like a caress. "Fourteen pairs of sash windows from London, sent ready made and glazed, along with spare glass for mending." His words held the deeply felt sound of love, much like the sound he made when he murmured sweet words into the pillow between them, words meant for her ears alone.

Why, Thomas Jefferson loved this place better than he loved anything or anybody in the world! It was there, plainly there, had been there all the time and she was only now aware of it. She needn't ever be jealous of European women, nor of other slaves, nor of his daughters. It was Monticello. This plantation was his real mistress. She heard it in his voice, saw it in his longing gray gaze. If a house was his true love then she must be in love with it too, must embrace it as if it were her own. That was the only sure way to bind this man to her forever.

She spoke to the rounded mound of her stomach. "You're home. You're at the 'little mountain' my tiny one. Life will be good for you here."

She smiled at the two girls as they entered the carriage once again. Martha smiled back but Sally saw fear in the girl's eyes, eyes so like her father's gray eyes. What was Patsy afraid of? Polly swept the musing from Sally's mind with her giggles and her questions.

"Sally, do you think my cousin Jack Eppes will be here?" She twisted to stare again out the carriage window. "Will it take long to get there?" The youngster tried to set her chipstraw bonnet straight but it kept falling down her back. "Did Father write to Aunt Eppes that we were coming home?"

"I don't know, dear. I'll ask."

Jefferson climbed into the carriage and reclaimed his seat next to Sally. He settled against the squabs and sighed. Sally turned to look at him.

"Thomas, will the Eppes be here?"

Jefferson moved close and murmured into her ear, his voice covered by the rattling of the rolling chaise.

"Sally," He cleared his throat, "Sally darling, we will have our own private rooms at Monticello. I want no one in our space but we two. You will care for our special place. Do you understand?"

She nodded and he smiled, then his face turned grave, his pale skin blanched under the freckles.

"One more thing, my love. Now we are back in Virginia you must call me 'Master' whenever we are with others...even the family." He again cleared his throat. "You must recall that things are different here than in Europe." She looked up into his icy gray gaze.

Suddenly she was reminded of a time when, as a nine year old she'd wakened on a cold, cold morning and Jimmy had told her the pond was all frozen over. Sally couldn't wait to see the ice so she'd dressed and had run all the way to the water...and he'd been right. The friendly water had turned into a sheet of gray ice. Exactly like Thomas Jefferson's eyes at this moment.

At the edge of the pond Jimmy had warned her not to go out too far on the ice. She'd ignored him. She just couldn't resist running madly toward the center of the frozen pond. Jimmy's shout hadn't stopped her but a crackling sound beneath her feet had frozen her in place.

Ahead of her the ice fractured into lines and angular circles. She looked at the ice at each side of her without turning her head. The black lines webbed and lengthened even as she looked.

"Easy." She could hear Jimmy's voice as if it came from far, far away. "Back up real easy, sister. Tiny little steps." Again she heard the loud crack of shattering ice. "Come on, girl. You can do it." Her brother's voice was the only good thing left in her morning. She'd followed his voice all the way to safety that day. Now she needed him again.

All the veins in her body were filling with crystalline shards of ice. He spoke again. She was in a carriage. The voice wasn't Jimmy's. The voice again chilled words against her ear. The voice of her Tom. Of her Thomas Jefferson. No. The voice of her Master.

"Call me Master except when we are in our rooms, dear. You will remember, won't you, darling girl?"

She nodded again. He smiled.

"Did you tell her, father?" Martha leaned forward, her question half shouted over the noise of the carriage movement.

Jefferson nodded and Martha smiled at Sally also, then set her shoulders against the padded squabs and closed her eyes.

"Told her what?" Polly shouted. No one answered.

Somewhere. In her head? Maybe back in Europe? On the ship? Here? In this carriage? Somewhere. Somewhere it had happened and she hadn't even known. But now, at last, somewhere behind her, Sally could hear the echoes of the heavy voiceless clang of metal, as if prison doors had slammed shut, had closed her off from life, had shattered her liberty away.

"Master?"

Then that left only, "Slave."

AT THE PORTICO Jefferson stepped out of the carriage ringed by cheering, singing slaves.

"Master back."

"Yeah, he back, thank the good Lord."

"You safe home now, Master."

Jefferson turned and helped Martha, then Polly to alight. He hesitated a moment then held his hand up to Sally to help her down the carriage steps. The crowd stood curiously silent for three hushed seconds before they again sounded their cries of celebration and welcome to the master of Monticello. Betsy Heming stepped out from the crowd to embrace her daughter. Jefferson turned away as if he did not wish to see what was written on Betsy Heming's face.

"You're home now, Sally girl," Betsy murmured in her daughter's ear. "Your mama gonna take care of you, and your little one." She kissed Sally's temple just below the brim of the smartly tilted Paris hat Sally had chosen for the last part of her journey home.

Sally leaned into the arms of her mother and turned her face into Betsy's shoulder, not caring that the rose filled chapeau loosened and slid down the silk of her black curls. The new hat hung against her back from knotted pink velvet ribbons, which had earlier been tied in a careful bow just under her chin.

"*Je parle francais maintenant, maman.*" Sally's words were muffled against her mother's dark linsey woolsey dress.

"What you say, child?"

"I said, I speak French now, mama."

~ * ~